Anyone But You

A TWISTED LIT NOVEL

Anyone But You

Kim Askew and Amy Helmes

Merit Press

F+W Media, Inc.

Published by Merit Press
an imprint of F+W Media, Inc.
10151 Carver Road, Suite 200
Blue Ash, Ohio 45242
www.meritpressbooks.com

ISBN 10: 1-4405-7001-9
ISBN 13: 978-1-4405-7001-8
eISBN 10: 1-4405-7002-7
eISBN 13: 978-1-4405-7002-5

Printed in the United States of America.

10 9 8 7 6 5 4 3 2 1

Library of Congress Cataloging-in-Publication Data
Askew, Kim, author.
  Anyone but you / Kim Askew and Amy Helmes.
    pages cm
  Summary: In this modern take on Shakespeare's "Romeo and Juliet" set in Chicago, the
teenage daughter and son of two feuding Italian American families, who own competing
restaurants, fall in love.
  ISBN 978-1-4405-7001-8 (hc) -- ISBN 1-4405-7001-9 (hc) -- eISBN 978-1-4405-7002-5
-- eISBN 1-4405-7002-7
  [1. Love--Fiction. 2. Vendetta--Fiction. 3. Italian Americans--Fiction. 4. Restaurants--Fiction.
5. Chicago (Ill.)--Fiction.] I. Helmes, Amy, author. II. Title.
  PZ7.A8373An 2014
  [Fic]--dc23
                              2013032876

Cover image © 123rf.com.

*This book is available at quantity discounts for bulk purchases.
For information, please call 1-800-289-0963.*

For our grandparents.

ACKNOWLEDGMENTS

"I can no other answer make but thanks, and thanks . . ."
~William Shakespeare, *Twelfth Night*

Thanks to Merit Press's intrepid editor in chief, Jacquelyn Mitchard, for believing in us. Thank you to the talented team at Merit Press, especially Meredith O'Hayre, Ashley Myers, Bethany Carland-Adams, and Sylvia McArdle. We're grateful to our early readers, Gigi Hooghkirk, Marianna Fowler, David Johnson, and Phyllis and John Helmes, who provided us with invaluable feedback. Many, many thanks to our parents, siblings, and friends for their enthusiastic support, including a special shout-out to art director extraordinaire, Harriet Grant. Finally, we humbly submit our heartfelt gratitude to Amy's husband, Mike Fowler (aka Mr. Darcy), and our literary fairy godmother, Nicki Richesin.

CHAPTER 1

From Ancient Grudge Break to New Mutiny

I TOOK A DEEP BREATH and backed through the swinging stainless steel door, leaving the chaos of the kitchen and entering the hushed, dimly lit dining room. Our sound system piped in Dean Martin's "You're Nobody 'Til Somebody Loves You" for no less than the fifth time that night. What a horrible sentiment, I thought, surveying the all too familiar scene. I'd been working at Cap's, our family's Italian restaurant, since I was old enough to know a two-top from a four-top. Located one flight of stairs below street level, the eatery had been a speakeasy during the Prohibition Era, and still looked as though it would be an ideal spot for a clandestine rendezvous. The low arched ceilings might have made the place feel vaguely cryptlike were it not for the smattering of regulars and the remarkably nondescript tourists who came in for our house specialties, including our "world-renowned" deep-dish pizzas (though let's face it—practically every pizza joint in town liked to claim this distinction). A sign outside decreed the building, built prior to Chicago's Great Fire of 1871, a historic landmark. I knew if tonight didn't go well, our restaurant could be history, too—only not the kind that gets commemorated with plaques.

My arms were laden with plates, probably one more than I should have attempted. A thin film of perspiration formed on the back of my neck from the effort to keep everything from sliding to the floor. Glancing up at my intended destination—the coveted corner booth of the restaurant's elevated mezzanine—I saw my dad already standing there, turning on his legendary charm as if he were George Clooney's slightly less dashing stunt double. Correctly interpreting my visual distress signal, Dad excused himself and swept down the four steps to remove the plate of risotto precariously balanced on my inner elbow.

"Gigi," he said, hissing into my ear, "that was the mistake of a rookie waitress. On tonight, of all nights?"

"Sorry, Dad," I whispered back, following him back up the steps toward our waiting VIP.

"Never mind. Where's Mario?" he said, asking about our maître d'. (Did I mention our restaurant was older than "old school"?)

"With Chef. They're having a disagreement over the dessert. Chef told Mario that—"

"Never mind." My father groaned almost inaudibly as we reached our destination, the popular Monroe booth. A framed black-and-white photo on the wood-paneled wall above the table revealed the source of the sobriquet. In the picture, seated at that very booth, was the revered (even by diehard Cubs fans) New York Yankees center fielder, Joe DiMaggio, feeding a spoonful of spumoni to his then-bride, a laughing Marilyn Monroe. Though we usually saved the popular engagement spot for couples, tonight's guest was a chubby, middle-aged man in business casual, dining solo. He'd told my dad that he was a banker in from Boston for the week, but we knew differently. The minute he walked in the restaurant's leaded-glass front door, Mario rushed forward to seat him at the Monroe table before ushering everyone on staff into the kitchen for a group huddle.

"It's him," Mario said in near hysterics, his heavily gelled black hair cascading in molten volcanic waves atop his head. In one hand he held aloft a mug shot type of photo that had been tacked to the kitchen wall for the last three weeks. Not a Wanted poster, per se, though it inspired the same sense of apprehension. The pixilated photo had been e-mailed to us by my distant cousin Olivia, who knew a proofreader at the New York office of the famed restaurant ratings publication *Zwaggert*. This unassuming man, who'd made a reservation under the equally unassuming name (or was it a pseudonym?) of Jason Smith, was the reviewer who would be responsible for updating or, perish the thought, removing our entry in their iconic foodie bible. To my family's growing chagrin, locals and tourists both seemed increasingly inclined to spend their paychecks at the latest trendy spot rather than at a venerable neighborhood institution like ours. Making matters worse was an Internet rumor claiming that our secret marinara sauce was actually a well-known grocery store brand. This vicious lie had recently spread across restaurant review sites like a mutant virus. Coupled with the costs for upkeep and outrageously high property taxes, the truth was this: without our *Zwaggert* rating, we could no longer stay afloat. The restaurant my great-grandfather had opened more than half a century ago was on the verge of oblivion, and "Jason Smith" held our future in his pudgy little palms.

"Nothing can go wrong tonight," my dad had warned us, unnecessarily, or so I thought at the time. We had all nodded in complicity and prepared for the evening ahead as if for battle. Having sharpened his knives resolutely, Chef Angelo hunched over his prep station with all the intensity of a surgeon being forced to operate at gunpoint. Mario and Mom frantically inspected the glasses and flatware for stealth water spots. Even my notoriously wayward cousins set about their waiter and busboy duties with startling sobriety, plying our ancient waitress, Carmen, with double espressos to jolt her otherwise sloth-like step into high gear. We Caputos knew how to stick together, and nothing in life was more important to us than Cap's. It wasn't just our family business; it was our nucleus, the center of our existence. As much as I sometimes yearned to escape into the wider world, I couldn't imagine who I would be without this place, or what I would do if I didn't have it to come back to.

Subtly sizing up our important patron, I lowered the dishes onto his table, gave him what I hoped was an endearing smile, and made a quick retreat as my dad resumed conversation with the seemingly ambivalent reviewer. As I headed back down the steps and into the main dining room, I took in the scene around me with a more critical gaze. The dated decor was quaint bordering on cliché. Red-and-white checked tablecloths were topped with blood-red glass candleholders, in which tealights flickered. Raffia-wrapped Chianti bottles hung from the ceiling. The brick walls were barely visible, covered as they were in hundreds of framed photos featuring headshots of has-been Chicago "celebrities" and yellowed pictures showing what the neighborhood looked like back in the "good ol' days." We may have been stuck in the past, but fortunately we were busier than usual tonight, and most of the tables were filled. A few couples on dates held hands while they waited for their first courses to arrive. Several of the old-timers were there, too. My favorite cousin, Ty, winked at me as he leaned over to refill the water glasses for an older couple who came every Saturday night without fail. Other than Mario and Chef's typical stoveside spat over whether to serve our standard tiramisu or the more elegant *panna cotta*, things couldn't have been going any more perfectly.

As I think back on that unblemished moment of calm, it was almost as though I'd been watching everything from underwater, where it was all peaceful and floaty, only to surface during a raging thunderstorm full of sound and fury. It all began when a brusque male voice I didn't recognize shouted that one damning word: "Fire!" As if on cue, the obscenely loud smoke detector started wailing its ear-splitting tone. Ty and I exchanged concerned glances, then he raced toward the kitchen, colliding with customers who were trying to make their way to the front door. As this fiasco unfurled, the overhead sprinkler system gave an initial venomous hiss before showering us all with water. The diners in their exodus let out screams, some toppling over chairs in their hurry to escape. As I started toward the front of the house to help direct traffic, my black flats slid on the wet tiles, and I grabbed the brass rail on top of a nearby booth to catch my balance. You'd have thought we were all on a downward-listing *Titanic*.

"Gigi!" My mom shouted to me from the kitchen pass-through, looking frazzled but resolute through the unexpected rain. "Help Mario get all the customers out of the restaurant safely. There's no rush; no one needs to be trampled. The police and fire department are on their way. Let everyone know there's no danger."

"But what about the fire?" I pushed wet strands of hair from my face and looked around in dismay. "What set off the alarm?"

"It's not a matter of what," yelled Dad as he brushed past me, looking as angry as I'd ever seen him, "but *who*. I've got to go shut off the water. Let everyone in the dining room know their next meal here is on us. *If* we reopen for business, that is." He stormed off through the back hallway. The smoke detectors continued their obsessive shriek.

"You mean, there's no fire?" I shouted over the din to another of my cousins, Frankie, who was occupied in supporting the elderly Mr. Garcetti toward the front of the house. Frankie shook his head grimly, yelling back, "It was *them*!"

Them. I knew instantly whom he meant. Their pranks and petty sabotage were one thing, but this time they had gone too far. As I digested the news, a loud cry seized my attention. Spinning around I saw, sprawled at the bottom of the mezzanine stairs, the *Zwaggert* reviewer, Jason Smith. He was clutching his leg and writhing in pain. I dashed over to him and crouched down.

"Sir! Oh my gosh, are you okay?"

"Do I look okay?" he muttered through gritted teeth. Given the strange angle at which his lower leg jutted out on the floor, it was clearly broken. As the remaining customers exited through the front door, water continued to pour down on us, a baptism by false-alarm fire.

"We called 911. You shouldn't move."

"As if I could," the food critic groaned. "Can't anyone turn these infernal sprinklers off?"

"My dad's working on it," I assured him. "I'm so sorry! Here, wait one second."

"Not going . . . anywhere," he said, grimacing in pain.

I went to a nearby booth, grabbed an oilcloth tablecloth—at least the underside of it was still mostly dry—and spread it carefully over him.

"I'll stay with you until help arrives," I said, situating myself on the step next to him.

The dining room now resembled a still life portrait of abandoned bacchanalia. Pools of water had formed on the floor. Wine and water glasses overflowed like dozens of mini Niagara Falls. Abandoned meals sat bloated, while streams flowed in tiny rivulets off the tables. All of it, ruined. I used the sleeve of my white blouse to wipe the water from my face, and, if I was being completely honest, the tears from my eyes. It was true that tonight's incident had "Monte payback" written all over it—but why? Why did they have it so in for us? I wasn't oblivious to our restaurants' long-running rivalry, and my cousins never wasted an opportunity to trash-talk our rivals, who owned an upscale Italian joint three blocks away—but there was a big difference between "friendly competition" and malicious destruction.

The sprinklers and fire alarm both suddenly ceased—*way to go, Dad!* I offered Mr. Smith a tentative smile.

"Uh . . . refill on your water?" The soggy and crippled food critic was obviously in no mood for my lame attempt at humor, so I hugged my knees and fixed my gaze on the wall to my left. Nearly all of the treasured photos on our walls had been pelted with water, and I couldn't help but hope the flimsy frames were barriers enough to preserve them. I used the edge of my apron to wipe the glass of the photo nearest me, which hung two feet above the floorboard, too low to have ever caught my attention before. Two boys stared back at me from the black-and-white image. They were standing in front of an old-fashioned pushcart with their arms slung over each other's shoulders. Wearing identical white aprons and newsboy caps, they couldn't have been older than thirteen. What struck me most was the fact that the young men were grinning from ear to ear. Senseless as it seemed, these unknown faces angered me. How dare they smile so callously in the face of my family's ruin! In the lower right-hand corner of the picture, faint pencil markings scribbled in the white border told me when and where the image was taken: *The Chicago World's Fair, 1933.*

CHAPTER 2

She Doth Teach the Torches to Burn Bright

TWELVE YEARS OLD WAS TOO YOUNG TO DIE—
especially on some thrill ride at the Chicago World's Fair.
You simply couldn't trust that the guy in charge of the safety
switch had an IQ greater than a sock monkey. Or what if the
engineers had cheaped out on nongalvanized screws, and the
whole tin contraption was *this close* to crumbling like day-old
biscotti? I was justifiably cautious. Benny had a simpler way of
describing it.

"Sissy."

"I am not going up on that thing. You can't make me." Craning
my neck, I squinted into the sun. Rivulets of sweat, prompted
either by the June heat or my sudden panic, threatened to spill
down my neck into my collar. I swiped my skinny elbow across
my brow, attempting to mop up.

"C'mon, Nick," Benny said. "You're breaking my heart!"

"You promised me a naked lady, not a date with certain death."

"We'll see Sally in all her peach-bottomed glory soon enough,
but she doesn't go on stage for hours. Besides, I promise you, *this*
view will be just as good as *that* one. Well, almost, anyway. Trust
me on this."

Trust me on this. I'd heard that line a million times from Benny
and recognized it as a harbinger for trouble. My skeptical eyes

scrutinized the glass and aluminum "rocket car" trams suspended high above the two man-made lagoons perched on the edge of Lake Michigan. Snaking toward the entrance to the Sky Ride's elevator was a crowd eager to plunk down twenty-five cents to catch the million-dollar view of the colossal fair's expansive Midway, home to all of the expo's rides and amusements.

"We shouldn't waste five dimes on this," I said.

"Oh, does the widdle baby need to wide the ponies instead?" I could feel my cheeks flush.

"If we spend it all now, we'll have nothing left for tonight."

"We've got enough to spare. Thanks to me."

I'd been a neurotic namby-pamby this morning when Benny suggested we hop the turnstiles to avoid the fair's fifty-cent admission, but I had to hand it to him. My clammy palms aside, our stealth maneuver—which he'd been crowing about all day—meant we actually had money in our pockets to splurge on a few amusements, the main attraction (for us, at least) being the ample-bosomed goddess, Sally Rand. Her fan dances could make even the devil himself blush, or so it was said. Benny and I had only heard secondhand accounts of her mesmerizing undulations behind strategically placed ostrich feathers. Buoyed by our wanton imaginings of this burlesque beauty, we had weeks ago devised a plan to see her here in the midst of our city's epic extravaganza. Having scraped together what small change I could, I was racked with guilt. I knew better than to spend money on something so unsaintly, considering the minor miracles it took for Ma to pay our landlord each month. But that wasn't the only thing eating away at me this hot afternoon. While I'd never admit it to Benny, the prospect of our first girlie show had my stomach all in knots. For starters, two knobby-kneed kids were guaranteed to get booted from a burlesque show quicker than you could say "hoochie-coochie." I pictured my pal and I being hauled away by the scruff of our necks, some hard-assed cop notifying our disgraced parents. When I suggested this likely outcome, Benny merely offered up another customary "trust me," leaving my anxiety at an all-time high.

Because here's the thing: I *did* trust Benny. If he said he could get us into the show, then he would. Using his wit, his charm, or the face old ladies could never seem to resist pinching, he'd get us in all right—maybe even front and center. And that's what ultimately had me feeling shakier than a two-legged table: Me, at a striptease. You may as well drop an elephant onto an iceberg. I'd been trying to tell myself it was a triumphant rite of passage. I was a healthy, *almost*-adolescent male whose only real experience with the human female form had been pictures of the Venus de Milo and clinical images from our life sciences seventh-grade textbook. So to see a real naked lady with an actual head and complete appendages? A month ago, I was throwing around all kinds of twelve-year-old bravado at the prospect, but now that it seemed a certainty, I was feeling the jitters. On top of that, going twenty-three stories skyward in what amounted to a giant sardine container wouldn't help quell my growing nausea. I racked my brain for more reasons we should move along to some other amusement when Benny, as if reading my thoughts, shoved an index finger in each of his ears.

"I'm deaf to your excuses, so don't even start. Let's get in line." I inched into the queue with him, but didn't intend on staying.

"You go ahead, Benito," I said, clearing my throat after I spoke. "I'll just wait down here for you. Get a soda or something."

"Grow some hair on your chest, already," he said with a sigh, as if he sported anything beyond peach fuzz. "You're in the best clothes you own. If the worst happens—" He drew a finger across his neck, morbidly. "—at least you're casket-ready." He glanced down at the cuffs of my trousers, which hit about an inch too high above my ankles. "Prepared for a flood, too, I'd say."

"This from the boy who glued cardboard to the soles of his shoes this morning."

"Lay off." Benny looked genuinely irked by this reminder of how hard up our families were. "Someday I'll be richer than Wrigley. You can say you knew me when."

If confidence was any indication of success, this was probably true. Still, I scoffed and glanced again at the silver gondolas ferrying passengers back and forth over our heads. Arguing with Benny about the Sky Ride seemed to sum up our friendship in a nutshell. He was the one with his head perpetually in the clouds, while I was the grounded one. His antics were audacious, dazzling, and larger than life, whereas doorknobs and telephone directories were more intriguing than yours truly.

"Hey, you two jokers, inch forward!" A brusque, hairy, and well-nourished man in a fedora hat and rolled-up shirtsleeves had gotten in line behind us. Benny turned around pointedly and cocked his head at a forty-five degree angle, his unwarranted moxie on full display. As I cringed, Benny leaned closer to me, then said loud enough for the man to overhear:

"Looks like 'The Human Ape' escaped from the *Ripley's Believe It or Not!* show, Nicky. Who'da thunk a steady diet of bananas could account for such massive girth?" I clenched my jaw and glared at Benny. *Stop before you get us both killed.*

"What? We're *kids*. What can he do to us?"

"Move it or split," the man muttered, apparently unruffled by my friend's obnoxious remarks.

"Tarzan's getting impatient," Benny said. "Listen, Nick, forget the ride. This is *our* day. The only thing I want is for me and you to root up some memories we can tell our grandkids about some day. Minus the part about seeing naked bazoombas."

"Really? Because I can just picture bouncing those future tots on my knee: 'Kids, you should have seen the size of 'em!'"

"All I'm saying is, if you really don't want to do the Sky Ride, then we don't do it."

I was grateful to my pal for this out, but his kindness only left me more conflicted. I hated being the damper on his devil-may-care zest for life. He never held it against me, but I knew I was dead weight around his ankle rather than a proper sidekick. Why couldn't I have been more like him? Why did I have to be so *me*?

"I'm really sorry, Ben."

"Nah, cut it out." He gave my ear a flick—his way of being conciliatory. "I thought it might be good for you, that's all."

"Good for me how?" I wondered, rubbing absentmindedly at the sting he'd inflicted.

"I just thought being up there, getting to see how big the world really looks, you might . . . oh, never mind."

"I might what?"

"You might wake up, I guess."

I furrowed my brow, not wanting to admit that I knew exactly what he was talking about. "Aw, hell, Nicky," Benny continued. "You need to open your eyes. Live a little. Are you going to spend the rest of your life assuming the worst? Because the worst doesn't always happen. It usually doesn't, in fact. We're kids, we should be having fun."

"I'm *fine* with fun," I said. "I'm just not fine with *this* fun." Benny glanced off down the Midway and shoved his hands in his pockets.

"When you're ninety-years old, you'll regret what you didn't do more than what you did do. But never mind, what do I know?" he said, shrugging off our tension with a smile. "This is the World's Fair! We came and we saw, now let's conquer! We've still got to check out the trained fleas!"

At that moment, shrill feminine giggles erupted from the line of people waiting to ascend the Sky Ride elevators, and we both homed in on a group of young girls, indistinguishable in their straw cloche hats and pretty summer dresses. Naked ladies terrified me, admittedly. But fully clothed girls? Sure, I was interested. This group was worthy of a whistle (though I prayed Benny would refrain).

"Or," Benny murmured, nudging me in the ribs, "we could take Cupid's wings and fly?" My pal had a way of sweeping people up in his vortex, and though I was more resistant than most, his powers of suggestion were hard to resist. After all, Benny provided one thing I wasn't usually able to drum up on my own: the sense that something exhilarating could (and just might) happen. With his little lecture still gnawing at me, I reached into my front pocket and rustled for change.

"I'll go," I relented. "But you owe me."

We stepped into the elevator a scant few minutes later, and then I felt my stomach lurch as we ascended. Had I just made a decision I'd live to regret?

* * *

From my seat on the lower level of the gondola, I contemplated a screw in the ceiling, refusing to shift my gaze to the windows that surrounded me on all sides. I could hear Benny about six feet away, his face pasted to the glass as he prattled on excitedly. By my count, he had uttered the phrase "Jesus, Mary, and Joseph!" fourteen times since we'd been up here. The theme of the World's Fair was "A Century of Progress," which seemed a misnomer if ever there was one. Just because you couldn't see the bread lines and shantytowns from way up here didn't mean they'd ceased to exist. I gripped my thighs nervously with my hands, trying to tell myself this was just like the 'L' train—only *a lot more* elevated.

"Aren't you going to check out the view?" The voice coming from my right-hand side was high pitched yet delicate— encouragement enough for me to dart my eyes in her direction. I quickly glanced back at the ceiling, hoping my cheeks weren't as red as they felt. I remembered her from the gaggle of girls we'd seen standing in line. "Kittens," Benny had called them, as if he was some society gigolo. She'd been decidedly shorter than the rest of the group. From the glimpse I'd just gotten, she appeared to be around my age, and she was cute, in a Norman Rockwell kind of way. Cascading from under her summer hat were two ponytails the color of brass. They hung in perfectly sculpted ringlets, like springs. She had rosy cheeks and lips that looked poised to say something precocious. I sat like a complete clod, too paralyzed to make eye contact, let alone speak.

"Why'd you even come up here if you don't want to look?" Her question almost sounded like a challenge.

"Why aren't *you* looking?" I asked. She sighed and fiddled with a small pearl stud in her earlobe.

"My mutton-headed big sister and her friends told me to scram." She rolled her eyes and nodded her head toward the right side of the gondola, where five older girls were oohing and ahhing at the vista. "I'm pretending to sulk."

"Doesn't look like they care."

"Yeah, well, they're annoyed with me. At least, Trudy is. She's mad that Mother forced her to let me tag along. As if I want to hang out with *her*. So, you afraid of heights or something?"

I could hear Benny still running his mouth on the other side of the gondola and realized it was rare to find any girl, let alone a cute one, conversing with me instead of my Casanova counterpart. Moments like this? Well, they just didn't happen to me.

"I guess I'm a little afraid of heights," I replied after a moment or two, instantly mortified that those words had escaped my mouth. Why not just lift up my shirt and advertise my yellow belly?

"Our insides *would* turn to pudding if we fell," she confirmed, unfazed by her own dire observation.

"Uh-huh," I stammered, sounding about as eloquent as Frankenstein's monster.

As quickly as it had begun, our conversation came to a standstill. I knew it was my turn to volley back a retort, but my brain and tongue felt stuck in drying cement. Wishing I could psychically beg, borrow, or steal some witty remark from Benny, to whom they came as naturally as breathing, I glanced again at the girl. I wanted to tell her that her eyes were the same color as the blue hydrangeas in our window box at home, but that would have been totally cornball. With the image of "blood and guts pudding" ricocheting in my brain, I was rendered mute.

"Are you alone?" she asked, breaking the silence. "Seems like you're up here on a dare."

I pointed with my thumb in Benny's direction and waited for the imaginary hearts to come shooting like fireworks out of her head. Whenever a girl got her first glimpse of my devilishly handsome (even for twelve) friend, swooning was inevitable.

"Hmm. Got a name?" she asked.

"Oh, that's Benny," I responded. "I've known him all my life."

"Not *him*. *You*. I'm Stella." She extended her hand so that I might shake it. I wiped my palm on my pants, then obliged her as she continued. "It means 'star.'"

"Dominick," I said, all formalities, since the moment seemed to suddenly suit it. "It means, 'our Lord.'" Benny would have fallen on the floor, howling with laughter, had he heard me. I swallowed hard, hoping to calm the snare drum beating in my chest. Gee, she sure was cute. Instead of letting go of my grasp following our introduction, she laughed and squeezed my hand tighter.

"Well, 'my Lord,' we're almost back to the platform. You really should look out the window, just once, before the ride is over. Come with me." She stood and tugged on my hand with both of hers. Mesmerized by this girl's face—and our sudden physical contact—I allowed her to lead me as I trudged, practically sleepwalking, to one of the observation windows on the other side of the tram car from where Benny was standing.

I felt woozy, and involuntarily squeezed Stella's hand tighter while steadying my left hand upon the glass.

"Holy mackerel," I marveled.

Stella leaned her forehead against the windowpane, the garish sun illuminating the top of her straw hat as if she were wearing a halo.

"Be careful!" I stammered, prompting her to giggle again.

"Thank you for caring, but there's no chance of me falling. Try it, you'll see."

As if going in for a first kiss, I reluctantly inched my forehead closer and closer to the glass until it landed with a soft thud against the smooth warm surface. I inhaled deeply, allowed my shoulders to relax, and gazed at the truly remarkable view spread out before me. Eastward, Lake Michigan reflected like a giant looking glass as far as the eye could see. In the other direction was the bustling skyline of the nation's second largest city. The skyscrapers gleamed and sparkled like the imaginary Oz from the illustrated book I'd seen on a class visit to the Chicago Public Library.

"Made you look," she whispered next to me. "You're going to thank me for this one of these days."

Though I couldn't see her face, I glanced down, taking note of Stella's pristine black patent Mary Janes and white ankle socks. We were still holding hands. Her last comment implied that she expected the two of us would still be interacting at some future point in time. Or was I taking it too literally? Not that I'd mind, but it wasn't likely this girl with the fancy new shoes and pearl earrings would enter my orbit (let alone the Near West Side where I lived) once we returned to earth. Not, at least, unless I did something audaciously "Benny-like." As I contemplated this, Stella dropped my hand, and my heart sunk. An older girl who could only be her overbearing big sister strode up to her.

"Give me your coin purse, Stalactite," she demanded. "I've only got two dollars left."

It sounded like a fortune to me, but Stella dug in her heels.

"No. Mother gave us an equal amount. It's not my problem if you spent all yours on chewing gum and cotton candy."

"Mother said I'm in charge, which makes me the boss. C'mon, cough it up."

"Uh-uh." Stella shook her head resolutely, causing her sister to scowl.

"I can make you."

"I can scream."

"I hate you, brat. Why don't you just *get lost*?" Trudy turned on her heel and stormed off to the far side of the gondola again. I looked at Stella's face and saw the fire in her eyes turn to sadness. I felt instinctively compelled to change that.

"Have you been to Paris yet?" She looked up at me, with a bemused expression. "You know." I pointed toward the ground way too far beneath us. "The Streets of Paris. Down *there*."

"Oh," she said, realizing I was talking about one of the fair's more popular international pavilions. Over a dozen countries were represented, including France. "I haven't seen much of *anything* yet. Trudy the Terrible insisted on spending most of this morning fawning over all the babies on display."

"You mean the ones in the incubators?"

"Yeah," she huffed. "All they did was sleep. So much for World's Fair excitement."

"Well, excitement just happens to be my middle name," I lied, my boldness increasing as I sensed the gondola bumping its way back to the platform. It was now or never. "I haven't seen Paris yet, either. Maybe you and I could . . . go together?"

"But my sister . . . ."

"Unless I'm really confused on what 'get lost' means, I think she just told you to disappear. Am I wrong?" A sly grin instantly took hold of Stella's girlish face.

"Wouldn't it be sweet revenge if I *did*? Get lost, I mean? With you?" Now she was the one who blushed. "But your friend—he might not want some girl tagging along."

"Oh, no—you won't be tagging along. And he won't mind. Just give me five minutes to talk to him." The gondola doors opened and our fellow passengers began to exit. I saw Benny threading his way over to me. "Go on ahead, and when you get off the elevator, give your sister and her friends the slip. I'll meet you behind the shooting gallery in the arcade."

"Promise?"

"I swear—on my favorite baseball card, in fact. That's as good as a blood oath."

* * *

"What do you mean you want to split up? Right now?"

"Yeah, Ben, like I said, I met a girl. A really *nice* girl. And cute, too."

"I saw you chattin' up that powder puff on the ride, but come on, Nick. You just met her. We've been talking about this day for months. This wasn't the plan."

"We have a *pact*." A year ago when Benny and I first began to realize that girls were not, in fact, carriers of the dreaded "cootie" scourge, we both agreed either one of us could give the other the boot to pursue *l'amour*, no questions asked. "You've cashed in pretty much biweekly for the last six months," I added.

"Quit exaggerating."

"Remember Abigail? Anna? Then let's move on to the Bs—"

"The difference is, I never asked you to honor the pact at the World's Fair, for crying out loud! *Here*, Nicky? *Today*, of all days?"

"We had a deal. I've always honored it, now it's your turn. C'mon, you wanted me to go on the Sky Ride, and I went. Do something for me, for once." I regretted those words the minute I said them, but it was too late to take it back. I sighed and hung my head. "Twenty minutes ago, you were telling me I'd regret all the chances I didn't take. You were right. I don't want to have any more regrets, starting now."

"You'll regret this," he said quietly.

"Just a couple of hours, that's all I'm asking." Part of me did feel guilty, but it wasn't like Mr. Personality ever had any trouble fending for himself. By the time we crossed paths again, he'd probably have amassed a harem of female admirers.

"I can't believe you're ditching me for some Dumb Dora."

"She's not dumb. And I wouldn't even ask except, well, there's just something about her."

"Oh, what? Newly-minted loverboy thinks he's just met his future wife or something? Guess what, Nick: We're *twelve*. Quit acting all moonfaced. You're not going to end up 'happily ever after' with the first girl who plucks your heartstring. Trust me on this."

"Okay, I see what this is all about." I folded my arms defiantly. "I was never supposed to invoke our sacred 'pact,' was I? No girl in her right mind would ever look twice at, *me*, huh? It was all just for you. That pact was just your way to get rid of the third wheel."

"I never called you a third wheel."

"But don't deny that's what you thought. I cramp your style, don't I?"

"Nick, just cool your heels."

"To hell with you. I'm outta here."

"Some friend *you* are!" Those were the last words I heard before my left eye exploded into lightning bolts, my head cracked the pavement, and my world went black.

When I came to, I was lying on my back staring up at a dome of concerned faces, and Benny's was among them. Had I fallen from the aerial tram car? If so, how could I possibly still be alive? A few ladies' fans hovered inches from my face, and I batted them away as I sat up and shooed off the gawkers.

"Cheesy Petes, Nick, thank God you're okay," Benny looked chagrined. "You weren't responding."

"How—how long have I been out?"

"You know this hooligan?" asked a balding middle-aged man, neglecting to answer my question and thumbing his finger at Benny. He handed me a paper cone of water that had been passed to him. "He's the one who clocked you, but he won't scram. Want us to flag down a policeman?" I took a cool swig and eyed my obviously contrite friend. He'd punched me? My memory of the incident was scattered around the inside of my brain like pieces of a jigsaw puzzle.

"I'm so sorry, Nick, I didn't mean to do it. I wasn't even thinking when I hauled off and—"

"Stop." My head was throbbing. "I'm fine," I said, transitioning to my feet to prove that everyone could just mosey along. Slowly people began to disperse, mumbling advice about cold compresses and seeing a doctor.

"He's probably still seeing stars," said one concerned older woman to her friend. Stars? *Stella!* I grabbed Benny by the elbow.

"What time is it?"

"How would I know? Around lunchtime, I guess."

"How long has it been since we got off the Sky Ride?"

"Twenty, maybe twenty-five minutes?"

I bolted toward the arcade, praying I wasn't too late.

CHAPTER 3

It Is an Honor That
I Dream Not Of

"AW, C'MON, GIGI, GIVE THE GUY A CHANCE."

"Dad, Perry Beresdorfer is just . . . ." I wasn't quite sure how to put it tactfully, so I shot my cousin Ty a "save me!" glance.

"He's a complete dolt, Uncle Benj," Ty intervened. "His idea of Parmesan cheese is that stuff in a green can. He thought *cacciatore* was our fish of the day!"

"He even wears pleated-front pants!" I added as an afterthought, albeit an important one.

"What's wrong with that?" Dad questioned, his brow furrowing as he unfolded his napkin into his lap for dinner.

"Well, it's just that, umm . . . ." I fidgeted in the formal, straight-backed dining room chair.

"No self-respecting adolescent male would be caught dead in *slacks*," my seventeen-year-old cousin Enzo completed my thoughts.

"I don't get it," said Dad, mystified.

"Which, with all due respect, Uncle B, shows why maybe you shouldn't play matchmaker for Gigi," reflected Enzo's fraternal twin, Frankie. Across the table, Dad gave him one of his don't-push-your-luck scowls, and I made a mental note to privately thank my brazen cousins for having my back. Despite their lobbying on my behalf, I didn't get the sense that Dad was going to abandon his campaign to, dare I say it, pimp me out.

"Well, anyhow, we *have* to invite him to your Sweet Sixteen party, honey," Mom said as she served a spatula full of lasagna onto my father's plate.

"Which we're *not* wearing nooses to, by the way," declared Enzo, reaching across the table for a garlic roll. Seated next to him, his mother, my Aunt Valerie, swatted him upside the head.

"You sure as heck *will* wear a tie, if that's what Gigi wants," she said. "This is her big day, and you three boys will wear hot pink sequined leotards if she says so."

"Only Enzo has the runway walk to pull that off," Frankie smirked, punching his twin in the bicep. "Just as long as you don't make us dance with the ugly girls, Gig."

"Don't worry, bro, she'll be far too busy dodging Perry, like that cartoon cat stalked by Pepé Le Pew," teased Ty, kicking me under the table. Sometimes it seemed as if every word out of my cousins' mouths caused a corresponding knee-jerk movement of their fists, elbows, and feet—bruise-inducing marionettes. Mom and Aunt Val had moved on to zealously discussing my birthday party decorations, while Dad, humming absentmindedly, reached his hairy arm clear across me to retrieve the balsamic vinegar. Enzo and Frankie had a thumb war match going even as their free hands shoveled forkfuls of dinner into their momentarily silent mouths. Carmen—not related to us by blood, but considered family since she'd been working at Cap's before my dad was born— was slipping contraband morsels of lasagna under the table to our German Shepherd, Sampson, whose exuberant wagging tail thudded against the table leg. As usual, our Monday night family dinner was more three-ring circus than civilized supper. Having experienced these get-togethers every week of my life on the one night in seven that our restaurant was typically closed, I could totally identify with Alice's bewilderment at the Mad Hatter's tea party. How in the world did I share the same DNA with all of these baffling personalities?

"I don't even want a Sweet Sixteen party," I sulked, stabbing at the leaves in my spinach salad. It felt as though I'd suddenly (and without cause) been branded the girl who longs for an occasion to spray tan, wear glitter hairspray, and behave like a raging prima donna. That *so* wasn't me, and the fact that my parents didn't realize it set my teeth on edge. Having given me life and then lived in my presence for sixteen years, it blew my mind how woefully they failed to comprehend me.

"We've been over this a dozen times, sweetheart," said my dad. "A big to-do is just the sort of thing we need to let people know we're back in business." Cap's had been shuttered for nearly a month to deal with the water damage.

"Then call it a 'Grand Reopening' or something. Why do you have to drag my birthday into it?"

"Because not even the Montes would dare rain on a sixteen-year-old girl's parade, no pun intended," Mom explained.

"So I'm the decoy?"

"You're our insurance," Aunt Val clarified. "We can't risk them pulling any stunts the first night we're back in business."

"If you ask me, you ought to get even with those bastar—sorry, Ma—*jerks*, for what they did to us. They should have to pay," Frankie said.

"I could make them pay," Ty stewed, flashing dark eyes the color of coffee grounds. "Just say the word, Uncle Benji."

"Yeah," added Frankie, "even Carmen here could roll up on that cocky, pretty-boy son of theirs, not to mention the pathetic entourage he calls friends."

"I won't specify exactly what I'd do to Roman Monte's face," issued Enzo, "but it might resemble Aunt Nora's lasagna here by the time I'm through with it."

"That's enough," said my mother. "Last I checked, our name was Caputo, not Capone."

My experience with Roman Monte was limited to hearing him nominally categorized as "Spawn of Satan" by my hyperbolic cousins, who claimed, among other things, that he had an ego the size of Soldier Field. I'd never laid eyes on the guy. Natural curiosity led me to wonder whether Frankie's assertion that he was a "pretty boy" had any merit, but I figured my cousins couldn't be counted on for a reliable answer on that front. I'd have to cyberstalk the guy when I had a chance and see for myself. Too bad Mom already planned on monopolizing my every waking minute for the next two weeks to help her pull off the birthday soiree I'd just as soon skip.

"What makes you think Roman Monte is the one who pulled our fire alarm?" I asked no one in particular. "Did anyone actually see him?"

"Seriously, cuz, don't be so naive," Ty sighed.

"What?" I continued. "Enzo, you and Mom were in the stockroom, and Chef was manning the stove. No one ever ID'd anyone, and—"

"Believe me, if we had proof, that family would be drowning in legal bills right now," said my dad, dismissing my point out of hand. "The new security cameras went in last week. Next time they try something, we can sue them to the hilt."

"Is anyone going to ever tell us the *real* reason our families hate each other, anyway?" I said, attempting a different tack.

"Because they're base degenerates," offered Aunt Val, most unhelpfully.

"I mean, there are plenty of other Italian restaurants in Chicago," I continued, "so where does all this hostility originally come from?" You'd think, being taught from birth that the Montes were our sworn enemies, I would already have a good answer to this, but I didn't. Our family had simply espoused this truth for as long as anyone could remember, which is why my question elicited only blank stares from the faces across the table, as if I'd just asked them to recite the world capitals in alphabetical order.

"Just steer clear of the lot of them. That means *all* of you," my father decreed, eyeing Ty in particular. Ever since the boys' dad, my Uncle Greg, had suffered a heart attack and died four years ago, Ty was like a simmering pot, always ready to boil over. "If there are any scores that need settling," Dad continued, "that'll be something that's handled directly between me and Joe Monte."

Carmen had a tendency to lag thirty seconds behind in whatever conversation was going on, but I half suspected the old lady could mop the floor with the rest of us, mentally speaking. Leaning closer to me, she whispered cryptically, "If you go digging up dirt, you'd better be sure you really want to see what's buried underneath." The wizened waitress had worked at Cap's longer than any of us. Did she know something more about our family's epic grudge that she wasn't saying? The only thing I could say for certain was that my cousins and the other part-time waiters and busboys we had on staff at the restaurant weren't exactly lobbying for a peace accord with our not-so-friendly competition. I had to wonder if any of them might have done something to incur this latest act of war. They were always puffing out their chests to one another about what they could do to mess with the Montes. Had they done something first? Was the fire alarm stunt an act of reprisal?

Mom dabbed her napkin at the corners of her mouth, careful not to mar the coral lipstick that had long been her signature shade.

"Security cameras," she said, eyeing my father. "That sounds . . . expensive."

"Rich thought it was a good idea," Dad explained. "Thinks it'll protect his investment." Perry Beresdorfer's dad, Rich, a venture capitalist who worked in an office building down the street, was a long-standing patron of Cap's. He had approached my dad following our latest debacle and offered to front the money we needed to get the business back up and running. It was a loan, of sorts, but not without a catch. Rich Beresdorfer naturally wanted ownership in the business as recompense for his generous contribution to the "Cap's Clean-Up Fund." Once my dad got our business back in the black, he'd purchase Rich's shares, plus interest. The whole thing sounded a bit squirrelly to me, but Dad had been acting a lot more optimistic—cautiously happy, even— as a result of this arrangement.

"Speaking of that whole nightmare, I finally heard back from our *Zwaggert's* critic," Mom said. "His leg's in a cast, and he's not exactly a bucket of sunshine, but I don't get the sense he's going to take legal action or anything."

"Okay," Dad sighed, "but what about our *Zwaggert's* rating?"

"Well, I didn't go there with him, obviously," answered Mom, who tended to handle things with more delicacy. Though no one voiced it aloud, we were all thinking about the fact that a cable foodie network had just crowned our rivals' restaurant, Monte's, as having the best deep-dish in the city. It was another foreboding indication of our eatery's dwindling cultural relevance.

"So, Gigi," said my Aunt Val, changing the subject, "is there anything special that you want for your birthday?"

"A restraining order against Perry," Ty suggested. I couldn't help but smile and nod in agreement at my favorite cousin's quip. As different as he and I were, he always looked out for me—though I got the sense that, like an overprotective big brother, Ty didn't want me interacting with *any* potential suitor, dolt or otherwise.

"You be nice to that boy, Gigi," Mom snapped. "His dad is holding our purse strings."

"No pressure, or anything," Enzo said with a snort. "You're lucky they're not planning your wedding to that sledgehammer."

" . . . *yet*," Frankie said. As usual, getting a word in edgewise among this crew was an exercise in futility. I often wished I could just say what was on my mind as effortlessly—callously, even—as my cousins did, but this family didn't seem to have room for me, the youngest, to be as outspoken as the rest. I finally piped up when everyone else at the table was officially mid-chew.

"Can I at least assume I won't have to cover tables the night of my party?" I asked. Nights off were a rare treat for me. My sorry social calendar would make cloistered nuns look like party girls by comparison. Of course, I had a few close friends from the all-girls Catholic school I attended, but as confidantes go, I was tighter with Cap's "fifty and fabulous" head chef than with most people my own age, which only goes to show how much time I actually spent in our family's restaurant. God, I needed a life, but sadly, it seemed nowhere on the horizon. As for prospects in the boyfriend department, well, notwithstanding the dreaded advances of Perry Beresdorfer, my options were sadly limited. Aside from the occasional cute boy who came in with his friends or family (and what was I going to do—leave my number on the check?) the only guys I knew worked at Cap's, meaning they were related to me or may as well have been.

"Waiting tables, no—but you'll need to work the room," Dad responded to my question. "Make sure you chat up everyone, especially the adults. And for God's sake, plaster a smile on your face. No Cranky Pants pout like the one you're giving now."

Even though I was annoyed that my parents were inviting scores of random business acquaintances and their kids—people I'd barely met or even knew existed before the guest list had been drawn up—it would at least fill the restaurant and keep me from looking like a total charity case, socially speaking.

"This is a day we want you to enjoy, Gigi," Mom said. I could tell she was being completely sincere. "Wow, it's like just yesterday you were my baby, and now, you're practically a woman."

I waited for my cousins to crack some joke about my bra size and was relieved when they failed to do so, each too distracted by the slabs of Aunt Val's cheesecake on their plates.

"You're going to have a wonderful night," Dad promised, "and just remember, this is all for you." He wasn't just talking about my birthday, and I knew it. Time and again, he had reinforced this assumption that I'd someday follow in his footsteps as proprietor of Cap's. It was a baton I didn't want handed off to me, but saying so would break his heart. Watching the way this business had left him exhausted, bitter, and financially broken, only a masochist would volunteer to be his successor. Yet, I couldn't be the one who ushered the family's legacy into extinction after four generations. There was a time I hoped that one of my three cousins might carry the torch, but my dad considered them complete knuckleheads (not entirely without reason). I, on the other hand, was the "anointed one" who made my parents certain, with each straight-A report card I received, that I was born to carry on Cap's tradition. As if sensing my thoughts, my dog, Sampson, settled his warm muzzle on my knee in sympathy. I stroked his velvety-soft ear under the table and gave my dad a small, but sincere, smile of appreciation. He meant well. Although hopes and dreams not centered around the yeasty aroma of baked pizza dough certainly flourished in my brain, they would never take root in reality. No number of birthday wishes could change that.

CHAPTER 4

Is Thy News Good or Bad?
Answer to That

BY THE TIME I GOT BACK TO THE FRONT STOOP of the humble apartment building where both my family and Benny's lived, my feet were throbbing more than my shiner. I'd spent all day and half the night looking for Stella, but it was hopeless. When I'd arrived, breathless, at the arcade, the cacophony of bells, whistles, kids' screams, and barkers' baritone yawps made me feel disoriented. Maybe I was still reeling from Benny's knuckle sandwich. Once my brain adjusted, it was pretty obvious: there was no trace of her.

At the shooting gallery, a grizzled man with a face like a wild boar gave me the once over. He looked relatively in charge, so I asked him if he'd seen a girl fitting Stella's description.

"Yeah, I seen her," he said, reaching with a hook for a stuffed purple cat, a prize for someone who'd just hit the bulls-eye. "She was standing around here looking like some lost sheep that stumbled into a pack of wolves. She circled the place for about fifteen minutes, till my boys started razzin' her. I guess she got spooked."

"Did she say where she might be heading?"

The man laugh-snorted, spit a chaw of tobacco onto the ground, and turned away. The only other place I could think to look for her was at the Paris pavilion. I walked and rewalked every faux cobbled *rue*, past the sidewalk cafés and beret-bedecked accordion players. Around every corner were suggestive nude drawings and lewd novelties for sale. This was where Sally Rand would be performing later, I realized, mortified that I had actually asked Stella to let me bring her to this den of iniquity. If she'd come this way, she'd surely have already run off, horrified. I spent the rest of the day combing the crowds, my eyes peeled for any sign of her, but my search was pointless. Trying to find her among the teeming throngs was like trying to wish the dead miraculously back to life. I scoured the children's Enchanted Isle and the Hall of Science, toured futuristic model homes, and even the two dozen yawn-inducing corporate pavilions. I double-checked the incubator display on the off chance she'd reconnected with her sister. No dice. I'd seen the World's Fair, all right—every square inch of it, but it had been a fruitless search, not a day of amusement. I'd fallen in love (yes; I'll say it) only to let it slip through my fingers. My best friend had belted me as if he were heavyweight champ Primo Carnera (Ma was going to shriek when she saw my face). Benny and I had banked on this being a banner day, and instead, well, it basically belonged in the crapper.

I dreaded the climb up three flights of stairs to where I knew my mother was waiting. Depending on her mood, she'd either skin my hide or giddily demand a second-by-second account of my day. I couldn't stomach either, so I collapsed onto the wooden stairs in front of the building. Scrutinizing my shoes to see how much damage they'd incurred over the course of the day, I heard the sound of a can being kicked down the street. The clattering object came to a stop near my feet. I looked up and saw Benny leaning against the iron fence post. In the moonlight, the front of his white T-shirt appeared drenched in blood.

"Any luck?"

"With what?" I muttered.

"Finding her."

"What do *you* think?"

He leaned in to get a gander at where his fist had landed.

"Yowza. Can you even see out of that eye? That's going to leave a mark." Leave it to him to crack wise about having pummeled me.

"Congratulations. The world finally has evidence of your brute strength."

"So, whaddaya say we do it all over again tomorrow?" More jokes. I wasn't buying.

"Whaddaya say you shove a sock in it?"

"Geez, Nick. I'm sorry. I'm really sorry. You look kind of mobster tough with it, if you ask me."

"I'm not mad about the black eye."

"The girl?" he asked. I nodded, glumly.

"I had no idea, honestly, how much it meant to you. Now I do. But, hey, you met a cute girl who thought you were the cat's meow. There will be loads more where she came from."

"But not *her*. She must think I ditched her, that I'm just some louse who lied to her." Benny sighed and kicked the tin can across the street with the flair and flourish of a professional placekicker. Then he turned back to me.

"It's my fault. Tell you what: I'll find her for you."

"I spent all day looking for her, Benny. It's done; she's gone."

"*I'll find her for you.*"

"You don't even know what she looks like."

"I got a glance," he shrugged. "What's her name?"

"Stella. Like 'star.' You're never going to find one star among millions. Besides, I don't even know her last name." I gazed up toward the sky for a moment, then glanced back at my friend. "What's the story with your shirt, by the way? Did you come home by way of the Union Stock Yards?"

"It's not blood, it's marinara sauce," he responded. "Which reminds me, I'm starving. Come up to my place for some of my ma's cooking, and I'll explain everything that happened to me after you left. You won't believe my good luck. It's *incredible*." Leave it to Benny to have had a wonderful, remarkable day. As we climbed the front stoop, Benny threw a reassuring arm over my sagging shoulders.

"It may take a little while, but I'll find her for you, Nicky," he repeated. "Trust me on this."

* * *

"Thanks, Mrs. Caputo," I said, as Benny's mother cleared our plates from the table. Out of politeness I forced myself to down the last morsel of her normally mouth-watering linguini with clams. The dish tasted the same as always, but for some reason I didn't find it as tempting tonight.

"*Ay, bambino,*" sighed his mother in exasperation as she sized up her youngest in his high chair. He appeared to be wearing more of the pasta than he'd actually eaten. Three of Benny's other younger siblings were in the adjacent living room, apparently engaged in some version of Greco-Roman wrestling, complete with shrieks and loud thuds. Let it be said that life was never dull at Benny's place. As an only child, I was ever amused by the nonstop cacophony in the Caputo apartment. "You know, Dominick, you're welcome here anytime," Mrs. Caputo remarked, ruffling my hair as she passed behind my chair with two more plates. "Are you sure you don't want a cold compress for that bruise?"

"No, ma'am."

"You need to be more careful," she warned. "Watch where you're going or you're liable to really hurt yourself next time."

"Yes, ma'am." I shot Benny a glare, but only in jest. We'd agreed on the way up to his family's apartment that it would be better to tell his parents and my mother that I'd inadvertently fallen headfirst into the street after tripping over a tree root. It was easy to blame it on that, since I had a reputation for being a klutz. Benny, as usual, was already on thin ice with his father, and a "street brawl" wouldn't do him any favors in the filial relations department.

"And you, young man." Mrs. Caputo, as if reading my thoughts, looked over at Benny, shaking her head in displeasure. "What's your excuse for coming home in that sorry state? It will take me hours to get those stains out."

"If things work out the way I think they will, Ma, soon you'll be able to send the laundry out to old Mrs. Speranza."

"Never mind. You'd better finish up quick and go change before your father gets home."

I was dying to know what Benny was up to, yet I didn't want to give him the satisfaction of urging him to spill it. While I bore him no malice for clocking me, I was still nursing a grudge about Stella. I wondered if I'd ever be able to completely forgive my best friend, even though there's no way he could've understood the depth of my feeling. Heck, even I didn't quite understand it. The only thing I could equate it to was *King Kong*, the movie Benny and I had seen under the elaborate dome of the Uptown Theatre. At the time, I'd been mesmerized by the gaudy opulence of the picture palace—meant to help us all forget for a few hours the Depression waiting just outside the threshold—and thrilled by the action and high drama of the film. It was only now that I had an inkling of what that giant hairy ape had felt for Fay Wray. Sure, I was twelve, but I was convinced I'd experienced what's known as love at first sight. Love at only sight, actually, since despite Benny's promise, it was doubtful I'd ever see Stella again.

"C'mon, Nick," he said, breaking into my thoughts, "hurry up and finish. We'll go talk out on the fire escape."

To us city kids, the fire escape was the equivalent of a tree house. We spent hours there, our legs dangling off the metal platform, as we waxed philosophic on everything from the batting averages of our favorite sluggers to the pros and cons of various superhero powers. We speculated on how far we might be able to spit from this high up and plotted our future careers, vacillating between Western gunslinger, flying ace, and submarine captain, the latter after we read Jules Verne's *Twenty Thousand Leagues Under the Sea*.

Benny and I had known each other since we were in utero, if you can count that. Our parents lived on the same floor of the building. His ma and mine had compared notes about their swelling bellies as they hung laundry to dry in the building's claustrophobic courtyard out back. Following our births (I came first, by three weeks), he and I were routinely shuffled back and forth across the third-story landing. Mrs. Caputo would watch me when Ma ran errands, and we'd take Benny whenever his mother had her hands full with his four younger siblings (which meant he was at our place more often than not). We romped our way through Hull House kindergarten classes together in matching sailor suits, and later donned black cassocks and white surplices as altar boys at Our Lady of Pompeii Church. Most of my childhood memories were infused with images of this pal of mine, from hours spent emulating Douglas Fairbanks in *The Black Pirate* to our lengthy discussions about if and when the White Sox might clinch the pennant again. Benny once told me that, until he was six years old, he thought we were actually brothers who lived in separate apartments. He was the Laurel to my Hardy, the Mutt to my Jeff, the Barnum to my Bailey. Despite the polarity of our personalities, we were frequently mistaken for fraternal twins. When my dad died a few years ago following a freak accident at the factory where he worked, people either looked at me with pity or avoided me outright so as to detour any awkwardness. Everyone but Benny, that is. His "business as usual" demeanor sustained me until I managed to build some semblance of a scaffold around my heart. Sure, we got on each other's nerves; spending as much time together as we did made it unavoidable. But today's fray seemed different; more indelible. It was fitting that we ended it, like so many other days before, on the fire escape, and that this was where Benny filled me in on the enterprise that was to become our life's work.

"*Pizza?*" I asked, repeating what he had just said. We had purchased our share of the tasty Italian specialty at "two cents a chew" from a favorite neighborhood peddler who traversed the streets of our neighborhood, distributing pizza from the metal washtub he carried on his head.

"Antonio says it's the food of the future," Benny said in response to my incredulous look.

"Who's Antonio, and what makes him the expert?"

"Aren't you listening?" Benny replied. "He's the pizza guy. I saw him at the fair. They're selling like hotcakes. He and his wife can hardly keep up with the demand, so he's expanding. That's where we come in. We'll be his apprentices. One of us will learn how to make the pizza while the other takes out Antonio's second cart. Then we'll swap. Here we thought seeing the Chicago World's Fair was a once in a lifetime opportunity. Now we're going to get *paid* to hang out there every day! Imagine all the excitement we'll get to be a part of!"

"How much will he pay us?" I asked, ever the pragmatist.

"A pittance, but what else are we going to do this summer? Once we learn the business, we can save up and break out on our own. Think of it: Benny and Nick's Pizza."

"Don't you mean Nick and Benny's Pizza?"

"Sure, if that's what you want."

"When do we start?"

"Tomorrow."

Sleep should have been my succor after the exhausting day I'd had, but that night I lay in bed tossing and turning. I was, of course, partly worked up over the anticipation of returning to the fair the following morning. The thought of getting to go to the greatest extravaganza on earth for the next few months—and get paid, to boot—was admittedly thrilling, but I couldn't manage to drum up the appropriate level of enthusiasm. Instead, my thoughts kept returning to Stella. I'd never had a girl as clever and beautiful as her give me the time of day. Holding her hand had been a high point in my life, and not just because we were umpteen stories off the ground. What a cad she must have thought me, to have left her hanging there, alone in that seedy arcade, when I had given her my word. I sat up in bed and clicked on the small lamp on my bedside table. My face still throbbed from where Benny's fist had made its mark. Reaching into the drawer of the nightstand, I pulled out my copy of *The Adventures of Huckleberry Finn*. There it was, still tucked between the pages at the beginning of Chapter Eighteen: My 1909 Honus Wagner baseball card. Nicknamed The Flying Dutchman, Wagner was one of the greatest shortstops in the history of the game. My dad had gotten this card from a pack of smokes in his younger days, and given our shared passion for the sport, it was one of the few items of his that I requested from Ma after he passed. Staring at Honus in his almost formal-looking Pittsburgh Pirates uniform against a gold background, I permitted myself to remember my father. It was something I normally didn't do, as it was just too painful. Dad had only been thirty-three years old when he died. This card connected me to him, far more than the framed photos Mom kept in her bedroom, or his World War I Victory Medal that we kept on display in the china cabinet. The card was scuffed around the edges from where Pops used to carry it in his wallet—"My lucky charm," he'd say— but I'd been treating it like the Holy Grail since taking possession of it. Benny was the only person I'd ever let have a glimpse of this small, personal treasure. Only he could understand the scope of its sentimental significance. I slid the card back into its berth at the start of Chapter Eighteen and returned the novel to my nightstand drawer, clicking off the lamp. Tomorrow was going to be another long day. I needed to sleep.

CHAPTER 5

Then, Dreadful Trumpet, Sound the General Doom!

"GIGI! IN THE NAME OF ALL THINGS HOLY—you're not even dressed yet!"

"Relax, Mom," I said, still wearing a green tank top and cutoff jean shorts. "It's just so hot back here by the oven. Unless you want me to wilt before I make my grand entrance, I'm not changing until the last minute. By the way, I'll start to smell like garlic if you keep me back here much longer." I patted my hair, which she'd carefully curled and set into an elaborate updo at the nape of my neck. The bobby pins jutting into my skull felt like tiny instruments of torture. Thankfully, after plucking a few wayward eyebrow hairs, she decided that caking my sun-kissed olive skin with makeup would be gilding the lily. I'd gotten off easy with just a bit of blush and some light pink lip gloss. My mother glanced at her watch, then pushed a stray tendril of hair behind my ear.

The simple ivory lace sheath she'd miraculously let me choose for this evening was still hanging up in its garment bag in the stockroom. Mom had compensated for my subtle choice by wearing enough glimmering rhinestones to outshine a Vegas showgirl, but despite our difference in tastes, she looked very pretty in her bedazzled cocktail dress. I could only hope to age so well.

"Oh baby, I'm so proud of you," she said, beaming. "Just be snappy when we call for you. It'll be another ten minutes or so, once we're sure all the guests have arrived. Angelo, will you make sure her bra straps are tucked in when she gets her dress on?"

"*Mom!*"

"Oh, for Pete's sake, Gigi, you know I lost any sense of modesty around Angelo on the day you were born." Chef didn't turn his attention away from the crostini hors d'oeuvres he was prepping, but I saw him raise his eyebrows in comic assent. To make a *very* long story short, he had ushered me into the world—right here on the floor of Cap's kitchen—when Mom had gone into labor with me during our Saturday night dinner service, three weeks earlier than I was due to arrive. It was clear Mom wasn't going to make it to the hospital on time, and since Dad was a total basket case, Chef had abandoned his post at the stove long enough to catch me in a flour sack kitchen towel. His nickname for me, to this day, was "Ladybird," because he said I had resembled a slippery plucked chicken in his arms. "And you squawked like a chicken, too," he liked to remind me. By the same token, I couldn't recall a time when I called him anything other than "Chef." Standing at the helm of Cap's kitchen wasn't just a job for him—it was, in many ways, his identity.

"In five minutes, I want you dressed and ready, young lady," Mom instructed, kissing my forehead. On her way back toward the dining room she paused at the swinging door and threw me a backward glance. "Perry and his father are here," she said with a sly grin. "He brought you a long-stemmed red rose! Isn't that *romantic?*"

I gave her a tepid smile, figuring this wasn't a great moment to voice my opposition. Discussing my unwitting love life with my mother made me inwardly wince.

Chef grabbed my shoulders and gently positioned me two feet away from the prep sink, where he was about to rinse some more tomatoes.

"Natalie Wood. That's who you remind me of, with your hair like that. Except she had brown eyes, and yours are that knockout blue from God-knows-where in the family gene pool."

"Natalie who?"

"Oh, child, I've gone and passed my expiration date, haven't I? All I'm trying to say is, you'd give any Hollywood starlet an ugly complex. Is this Perry who I think he is?"

"Yeah. The son of Dad's sugar daddy."

"Careful, Little Miss Lippy. That's no way to talk about your father."

"I know," I said, guiltily. "I'm just tired of everyone trying to sell me on 'Stare-y Perry.' He never blinks, by the way. Just gapes. Like a fish."

"It's the look of luuuuuve," Chef teased, doing impromptu fox trot steps as he shuffled his way over to grab the industrial-sized container of olive oil.

"Unrequited," I clarified. "*Quite* unrequited." I slid the pedicured toes of my right foot in and out of my rubber flip-flop sandal. "Loving someone against their will should be a crime, don't you think?"

"You're talking to the wrong Guido, doll. When it comes to romance, I'm about as hopeless as a dog trying to catch its own tail. But go easy on the poor sap. One of these days you might fall for someone you can't have, in which case you'll feel a bit more sympathy for 'Stare-y Perry.'" He picked up a clean metal spoon and scooped a bit of chopped tomatoes, basil, and olive oil onto it, presenting it to me for a taste. "More salt?"

"No. *Perfecto*," I said.

"Good, now you back me up on that if Mario starts in on one of his 'it needs more seasoning' rants. If he wasn't such a sourpuss, his taste buds might actually work correctly." Not wanting to enter the always comical "Chef vs. Mario" fray, I opted to change the subject.

"I'm sorry you have to work tonight."

"Zip it. You know I wouldn't miss your party, Ladybird."

"But I wish you could be out there—" I motioned to the dining room. "—not slaving away back here all night. I'd much rather be celebrating with you than with any of *those* people." I hugged him around his pasta-fortified middle, and he patted my head encouragingly.

"I know you feel like a fish out of water around here, but you're worth more to this family than all those priceless paintings at the Art Institute—even that avant garde stuff that just looks like scribbles. The people on the other side of that door might not always understand you, but you're the brightest star in their sky. Now go shake a tail feather! I'm scared of what your mother will do to me if you're not dressed and ready," he said, teasing. "And remember, at the end of the day it's only a birthday party. It won't kill you to try and enjoy it."

* * *

Mom and Aunt Val had mounted heavy black velvet curtains just beyond the swinging stainless steel door that led into the dining room, and I'd been instructed to enter the party through them after Dad had made my introduction to the guests. I could hear him speaking into the cheap portable microphone we had on hand for company banquets, wedding rehearsal dinners, and the like.

I was dressed and ready, waiting behind the curtain near wooden shelves we kept stocked with napkin rollups and oil and vinegar cruets. The balls of my feet were already starting to throb in my strappy silver high heels.

"Sixteen years ago, our beautiful, bright, and kindhearted daughter entered our lives in this very restaurant," noted my dad, eliciting a chuckle from members of the crowd familiar with the story of my birth. "Her mother, my wonderful Nora, was the picture of tranquility, but I kept running around the room screaming, 'Oh, gee! Oh, gee!' I think that may have been why Nora suggested her nickname be Gigi." Another round of laughter reverberated through the room. Dad ought to have trademarked this corny anecdote for as many times as he'd told it.

"Tonight," he continued, "we're beyond overjoyed to have so many friends, old and new, helping us celebrate right here in the same locale where we first met our daughter. This old neighborhood joint, which my grandfather first opened in 1945, is the Caputo family's lifeblood. Knowing it will be around, not just tonight, but for generations to come, means the world to me, and for that I say, *Salute*."

"*Salute! Salute!*" came cheers from partygoers, along with the sounds of clinking glasses.

"Which brings me back to Gigi, the reason we're all here," Dad said. "To know her is to love her, and we love her . . . very, *very* much. So without further ado, please help me welcome the Caputo family treasure, my remarkable birthday girl, Julietta Marie!"

As I pushed through the velvet drapery, the undeniably catchy (but admittedly over the top) sound of big band trumpet music started blaring over the restaurant's sound system. After some initial dithering a few weeks ago, Mom and Aunt Val had ultimately opted for a "swing era" party theme to commemorate the year in which Cap's had first opened, way back when. Given that our family considered tonight's festivities the restaurant's rebirth, of sorts, the theme had added significance. I'm sure most of the people my age at the party were going to think this music was geriatric, but, hey, it's not like I had any say in the matter.

Stepping into the dining room, I could see that the restaurant's lighting was dimmer than usual. Mom, having used to excess the word "classy" in the run-up to the party, wanted Cap's to resemble an old-school supper club, so she'd festooned the place with white ostrich feathers and a bazillion silver helium balloons. For tonight only, the red-and-white checkered tablecloths had been traded out for plain white linen, each crowned with a black tulip floral arrangement. A silver and gold banner hanging over the bar said, "*SWING* . . . Into Sweet Sixteen!"

"Gigi, sweetheart," Dad said, extending his arm toward me. He looked dapper in his white jacket and black bow tie. I walked over to him as the gathered guests cheered and whistled. I couldn't make out many faces in the glare of the spotlight cousin Enzo had rigged up for the occasion. Beaming and simultaneously embarrassed by the attention, I found momentary refuge in one of my dad's bear hugs. It would have been perfectly natural, in the moment, to tell him that I loved him, too, but I found it impossible to say the words. In recent years, my relationship with him had changed . . . or maybe it was only that *I* had changed. I appreciated my dad as much as ever—maybe more so, knowing how hard he worked to support our family and the business—but our relationship had become increasingly stilted, tense even. The more I tried to establish my own identity, the stricter he became in his edicts and absolutism, unable to allow for the fact that I might yearn to deviate from the master plan he envisioned for me. Dad had worked enough pizza dough in his life to expect that his only daughter would be just as easily pliable. With every tentative step I made to assert my own thoughts and opinions, I sensed a growing disconnect between us. He didn't want his "little girl" to go away, even as I so desperately needed to test the waters of adulthood. Though I couldn't exactly give words to any of these sentiments, I burrowed a little deeper into his chest to let him know that, despite my turning the big one-six, he wasn't going to lose me.

As the cheering subsided, I worried for a knee-wobbling moment that I'd be expected to utter words of some sort into the microphone as the guest of honor. I couldn't possibly give a speech—the very thought had me ready to bolt for the nearest exit. Luckily, Ty (who had appointed himself DJ for the night) had cued up a version of "Chattanooga Choo Choo," and people started sauntering back to the buffet table. I glanced around trying to find any of my friends from school, but Dad, his arm still around my shoulder, ushered me over to, who else: my unsolicited suitor and his father.

"Hi, Mr. Beresdorfer!" I said with as lively a smile I could muster. Talking to him reminded me of going to the dentist; painful, but necessary. "Thank you so much for coming tonight. And, uh . . . you, too, Perry!"

"Happy birthday, Gigi. You look pretty smokin' tonight." Lord. He handed me a single red rose wrapped in clear cellophane, a bright orange price sticker still stuck to the plastic.

"Oh, Perry, you shouldn't have," I said (by which I meant, *I so wish you had not.*)

"Fuggedaboudit," he shrugged, clearly unaware of how lame it was for people who were zero percent Italian to speak like a mafia don. "You chicks are suckers for flowers. And, well, I am nothing if not a gentleman."

I forced a pseudo-smile. He was wearing a blazer with gold anchor buttons on it and a giant class ring that looked like something won in an NBA championship. It was almost as if a mad scientist had morphed his baby face onto the body of an AARP member. My dad had the audacity to compliment Perry's novelty tie, which was covered with golf balls. (Dad usually referred to golf as a "game for putzes," but suddenly he was acting like he, too, had just emerged off the back nine.)

I wasn't sure what I was supposed to do with the rose now. Carry it around for the rest of the night? Stick it between my teeth and yank Perry into a passionate tango? (Dad would have been thrilled.)

"So, I guess this makes you legal now," Perry continued, with— ew—yet another Dad-inappropriate remark.

"Yep," Dad responded for me. "Trading in the learner's permit for the official state ID of Illinois pretty soon, eh, Gigi?" Oh.

"I guess," I answered. "If I pass the driver's test."

"Just what the world needs," laughed Mr. Beresdorfer, "another woman driver on the road. Better up the coverage on your car insurance, Ben." All three men laughed heartily. This whole macho-man conversation was to be expected from Perry and his father—but since when did my dad have to chime in? Was he going to start smashing beer cans on his forehead next?

"Don't worry, Ben," added Perry, knowingly patting my dad's shoulder. "I'll make sure I'm the one behind the wheel."

"In that case, just get her home by midnight, or *else*," said Dad pointing his finger in mock threat. Wait a minute. Were they under the assumption that I was ever going to be in a car with Perry? Like on dates? No. Just no.

Dad had started discussing business stuff with Mr. Beresdorfer, which left me conversationally stranded with his son, a boy who was about as interesting as burnt toast.

"So, uh . . . have you met any of my friends yet?" I asked him, craning my head to look for one of them to rescue me. Where on earth were they?

"Not really," he answered. "I don't know many people over on this side of town." Perry went to some private school in Oak Park that I'm sure cost more than some college tuitions. I couldn't tell if there was an air of superiority in the way he spoke about our neighborhood, but decided not to assume the worst. He already had enough strikes for him in the "Ugh" column that it wasn't necessary for me to find any reasons to add more.

"Okay, well, I'll try to introduce you to some people. My friends should be around here somewhere . . . ."

"No worries," he said, good-naturedly. "I'm thinking I'll just stick like glue to you all night. I mean, what's the point of doing the chit-chat thing with strangers, when I'm really here to hang out with you?" With that, any tiny remnant of hope I had that this party might border on fun vanished like an ant blasted off a driveway by a high-pressure hose. I craned my neck again to find my friends, looking past Perry's shoulder as he prattled on about his dairy allergy, of all things. My eyes had gotten used to the dark lighting by now, but I forgot all about the girlfriends I was supposed to be scouting when I saw a guy—a jaw-droppingly gorgeous guy, I might add—enter through our restaurant's back door. The way he'd sidled in, leading with one shoulder, reminded me of a stray tomcat slinking through a chink in some garden wall. He glanced around the room as if looking for someone—his parents, perhaps? My folks had invited so many random friends to the party that there was really no telling who he might have been connected to. Resting against a brick pillar, he dug both hands into the pockets of his dark denim jeans. A black skinny tie dangled insouciantly from the collar of his workaday white oxford shirt, the sleeves of which were rolled up to just below his elbows. His slouch mirrored the cool informality of his attire, and he studied the scuffed toes of his black Converse sneakers. Like the statue of David, his face looked focused and calm, yet poised for action. But I'd bet even Michelangelo couldn't have carved anything more perfect than this guy.

" . . . and while I *love* cannoli," Perry blathered, "they need to be filled with a soy-based cream." I nodded absently, never shifting my gaze from the boy standing ten feet behind him. Perhaps the boy sensed as much, for he slowly turned his head in my direction and looked straight at me, engulfing my chest cavity in flames.

" . . . it's not so much the lactose that's the culprit," Perry droned on, delving into the mind-numbing topic of whey proteins and shifting his body so that my preferred view was suddenly blocked. I sidestepped half an inch to the right and found his eyes again, to my sweet relief. I smiled, quite involuntarily, and was amazed to see the faintest hint of a grin echoed in his perfect face. I could happily have stood there frozen in time—even if it meant being forced to listen to Perry's dissertation on the perils of dairy. The only things I suddenly required in life were those angelic eyes, that devilish grin . . . .

"Earth to Gigi!" The voice of my friend Bethany ripped me out of my reverie, and I tore my eyes away from his. She was flanked by four of my closest friends from school.

"Oh . . . hi! There you guys are!"

"So, are we even going to get to hang out with you at all?" demanded another classmate, Anna Lopinsky, looking pert in her flouncy navy blue frock.

"Well, yeah, uh . . . of course!" I said, glancing back toward the darkened corner of the room. He was gone. Disappointment washed over me, but I tried to shake it off. "I was wondering where you guys—"

"Get together, everyone; I want to take a picture," Bethany interrupted, moving a few steps away so she could aim her phone in our direction. Like an unwanted fungus, "Perry No Dairy" sidled closer to me than the situation warranted, causing me to cringe. Though I didn't have the nerve to speak my mind to this insufferable swain, I conveyed my contempt for him more subtly.

"Okay, everyone," I said, "Say 'Cheese!'"

CHAPTER 6

What Light Through Yonder Window Breaks?

"BENNY—ISN'T THIS A LITTLE EXTRAVAGANT?" I asked, glancing skeptically through the storefront window. Workers had just finished hanging a large sculptural sign outside, perpendicular to our shop's front door. It was guaranteed to visually accost any and all pedestrians and motorists on the street. A giant red arrow blinked on and off intermittently, the words PIZZA PIES (spelled out in letter-shaped lights) making it abundantly clear what we were selling.

"It's neon," Benny proudly explained. "They call it 'liquid fire.' And if you think it's bright now, you should see the way it's going to look after dark. This is really going to get people's attention."

"By *blinding* them?"

"This is the future, Nick. Trust me."

I sighed and climbed off the stepladder I was standing on, setting my paint roller back in its tray. Despite the open door and windows, the paint fumes were getting to me.

"Don't get me wrong, I'm sure it'll cause a stir. But a metal placard would have been a lot cheaper. We've got to be careful with our funds, Ben. The pizza oven is setting us back a pretty penny, and you go blowing the budget on this?"

"Relax, Nick. Haven't you ever heard the expression, 'You've got to spend money to make money?'"

"Oh, now you're J.P. Morgan, spouting off financial wisdom? We're just a couple of kids who dropped out of high school to make pizza."

"And look where it's gotten us, my friend!" Benny smiled exuberantly, extending his arms to size up the small corner shop we'd recently leased. "Twenty-year-old entrepreneurs? Who'd have ever thunk it? Antonio must be smiling down on us, God rest his soul."

Our cherished friend and original mentor from that summer at the World's Fair, Antonio the pizza peddler had passed away three years earlier in a tragic streetcar accident. His wife, Vera, had been pregnant at the time with her first child, so Benny and I had stepped in to assume operation of the small pizza shack he had started, which was little more than a tin shed with an oven. Under Antonio's tutelage, Benny and I had become masters at slinging pies. The Naples-born immigrant's no-fail formula for a perfect crust and mouthwatering marinara proved a literal recipe for success, especially among the residents of the city's Italian enclaves who were homesick for a taste of the old country. Benny and I eventually quit school early and took over Antonio's business following his death. Although we were only seventeen years old at the time, we managed to make our modest profits rise at a slow but steady rate. As a result, we had money enough in our pockets to supplement our families' incomes and still provide for Antonio's widow and her baby daughter, Carmen. It had been Benny's idea to use the small savings we had amassed to open a bona fide brick-and-mortar location, which is how I came to be standing here painting over the pink walls of what was formerly a ladies' haberdashery near the corner of West Lawrence and North Broadway.

"Why is the top foot and a half of that wall still pink?" Benny asked in confusion, sizing up my incomplete paint job.

"That's as high as I'm going on the ladder," I said, wiping my brow on my blue denim coveralls, which were now speckled white. "I left the rest for you, so grab a paintbrush and make yourself useful."

"It'll have to wait," replied Benny, too distracted to mock my still unrelenting fear of heights. "I can't get paint on these duds. Got a girl coming over later."

"Of course you do," I said. "Only one this time?"

"No, actually, I threw you a bone and told her to bring her sister. You can thank me later, after you've sized her up. We can all go tear it up over at the Green Mill."

"And get shot up with Tommy guns?" I asked, facetiously. The Green Mill Jazz Club, spitting distance from where we were, was a known gangster hangout and speakeasy during the Prohibition Era. Al Capone's favorite booth was now practically a holy shrine there.

"The way I see it, all those 'wise guys' are our potential customers. We ought to mingle."

"Benny." I looked at him with exasperation.

"What? I'm *kidding*."

"I'm not. We're swamped with work here. Now's not the time to be chasing skirts and pretending we're hepcats."

"She's not just some skirt. And I'm not chasing her. We're in love."

I opened my mouth to speak, but nothing came out. I was slack-jawed. I'd watched Benny make time with a decade's worth of pretty girls. Like Chicago's leading Lothario, he'd spent his adolescence stealing (and squandering) the hearts of fair maidens with much the same enthusiasm that he'd exhibited as a child collecting fireflies in a jar. As with the bugs, his fascination for these young women dissipated the moment he had actually captured them. Going steady was never his aim—it was only the chase he found exhilarating. Needless to say, "love" had never even entered his vocabulary, so now that he'd uttered it for the first time, the word resonated in my ears like a ladle clanging the bottom of an empty spaghetti pot. Even though I was standing on the floor, I felt struck by a fleeting sense of vertigo, and reached for the push broom propped against a table to steady myself.

Benny leaned his back against the tile counter we'd installed last week and hopped himself to a seated position atop it.

"I know what you're thinking," he began.

"Am I that predictable?" I rested my chin on the tip of the broom handle.

"This is different," he said, ignoring my question. "I am done. Playing the field, I mean."

"Have you lost your mind?"

"Not any more so than usual," he joked. I walked over to him and placed the back of my hand across his forehead as if checking his temperature.

"Are you ill?" I wondered. He shook his head, grinning. Was he actually blushing? I clutched his chin in my hand and turned his face back and forth as if examining a melon.

"No," I said decisively. "This cannot be my friend Benito Caputo. He's been switched, under cover of night, with some sappy, starry-eyed Romeo."

"It's true, Nick. I love this woman."

"A *woman?!* Oh, thank God. I was worried that you'd fallen for some pack mule. But that's what you may liken your 'fair Juliet' to tomorrow when the next pretty girl turns your head."

"Not this time, Nick. Not anymore. She's smart, she's feisty, she's a real looker, and she's the one—I'm certain of it."

"*The one?*" I was incredulous. He smiled and nodded. "Well, for crying out loud, you old dope! I'm happy for you!" Prodding him in the ribs, I added, "In that case, I'm glad she's on her way over here. I've got to meet the nice Sicilian girl who finally nabbed the mythical Golden Fleece: your heart."

"Yeah. About that . . . ."

"Wait—don't tell me she's a *Genovese*. I might have to disown you," I teased.

"Funny thing, actually. She's not even Italian," Benny clarified, setting off more of my mental clanging.

"Now you're pulling my leg! Let me guess: Polish? German?"

"Neither. She's . . . not exactly from our neighborhood."

"The plot thickens," I replied dramatically, backing away from him and returning to my paint roller. "Papa Caputo's not going to be too keen on this."

"Tell me about it," he sighed. "I haven't told him or my mother yet."

"Remind me to vacate the premises when you let that cat—or should I say kitten—out of the bag."

"I know, I know. Ma's going to start crying that it ain't right with God. Dad's going to, well . . . I'm not sure whose father I should be more worried about, mine or my girl's."

Benny's musings were interrupted by the piercing sound of glass breaking and a small popping explosion. Our sign! We both ran to the front window and saw shards of colored glass raining down onto the sidewalk. The old wooden bowling pin that had struck the neon sign rolled off the sidewalk and into the street like a wobbly bandit making its half-hearted getaway. A silver-and-white Hudson Coupe squealed through the intersection just as some hoodlum hanging from the passenger window screamed, "Feed it to the Pope! We don't want you Sacco-Vanzettis around here!" (The pejorative referred to two Italian immigrants who'd been executed for armed robbery and murder in 1927.)

Benny yelled a litany of Italian curse words at the vandals as the car disappeared into the distance. A few pedestrians stopped and gaped. Still muttering under his breath, Benny spun on his heel and stormed into the kitchen.

I respected my friend too much to ever say "I told you so," but that didn't mean I wasn't thinking it. When we initially discussed opening a counter-service pizzeria, I had suggested a location in our home turf, somewhere on Taylor Street, where you couldn't walk two feet without bumping into a paisano. Benny disagreed with me, arguing that the best way to grow the business would be to introduce it beyond the sphere of Little Italy.

"That way, we expand our customer base—introduce a taste of Napoli to all the people whose last names don't end with a vowel," he said at the time.

"But the people you're talking about wouldn't know mozzarella from an umbrella," I'd argued. "You're banking that we can convert *them* into pizza lovers?"

"This isn't just any pizza. It's *our* pizza. One taste, and we'll have 'em eating out of the palm of our hands. Or *their* hands, I should say. We can't lose."

Since our calamitous (and, in many ways, fortuitous) first day at the World's Fair all those years ago, I had never forgotten Benny's criticism that I was too cautious, too afraid to take a risk. So while the pragmatist in me harbored serious doubts, I had buried them and agreed to set up shop in this swank section of Uptown, a good six miles north of our home turf. This was Benny, after all. I trusted him.

I swept up the broken glass out front. Benny spent about an hour in the back of the shop, shifting around wooden crates of cooking supplies while I finished up some detail painting along the floorboards. When he finally reemerged from the kitchen, he took a cross-legged seat beside me on the ground, looking more dejected than I was accustomed to seeing him.

"Well, you were right about the sign," I said.

"How do you figure?"

"It certainly attracted attention."

"I won't argue with you there," he sighed. "I'll figure out some replacement tomorrow. Guess a metal placard would be better, after all."

"No way." I shook my head. "Tell that neon sign company to make us a brand new one. Only *bigger*, this time. And brighter, if that's even possible." A slow grin emerged on my pal's face.

"What about the budget?"

"If we're going to do business on this end of town, we'd better *mean* business, too," I said. "Nobody's running us out of here. We'll take out a loan if we have to. Besides, didn't you know you have to spend money to make money?"

"Now who's the one not acting like himself?" Benny laughed, slapping me on the back so hard that I lost my balance and placed one hand into the can of paint I'd been using to touch up the trim.

"Watch it, wise guy!" I yelled, annoyed but laughing in spite of myself. I reached to smear my hand on Benny's face, but he grabbed my wrist and held it at arm's length.

"Unhand me, you dried herring!" I shouted, setting my mouth into a steely grimace as I issued my challenge. For as long as I could remember, trying to out-insult each other had been our favorite sport. Whoever balked during a quick succession of comebacks— or laughed first—forfeited.

"Flea-bitten gypsy!" Benny replied. Gritting his teeth and twisting my wrist, we simultaneously launched into an arm-wrestling showdown.

"Rank-smelling rapscallion!"

"Knobby-kneed gnat!"

"Pig-snouted . . . canker sore!"

"Sweat-stained scamp!"

"Clay-brained, Cupid-struck carbuncle!" My last remark prompted an uptick at the corners of Benny's mouth: an involuntary grin.

"Hey, can't a couple of girls get some service around here?" A feminine voice interrupted our horseplay as Benny, vanquished, released his grip on me.

"I win," I taunted him.

"No. *I* win," he grinned, pointing at the visitor who'd interrupted. "Estelle! You made it!" He bounded toward the front entrance to greet a young woman of indescribable beauty. Benny clearly hadn't been exaggerating his claims. I half-expected him to launch into a vaudeville-style song and dance number at the sight of her, but he seemed unexpectedly well-mannered around her.

"You must be Nick," she said, unclutching one gloved hand from the handle of her pocketbook and extending it toward me. I displayed my paint-covered right hand and shrugged. She laughed. With bright eyes and hair that framed her face in a glossy platinum permanent wave, she was an Art Deco goddess come to life. Her face mixed a screen siren's beauty with the placid serenity of those hallowed creatures in the copy of *Early Christian Saints* Ma kept on the shelf of her nightstand. "It's wonderful to finally meet you!" she continued. "Ben's told me so much about you."

"My apologies for that. I'm afraid I'm a terrible bore."

"Oh, that's okay. The coma only lasted a few days."

Wow. This girl didn't miss a beat, and judging by her bold red lips and the jaunty angle at which she wore her felt tilt hat, I got the sense she was no shrinking violet. Since I wasn't sure to what extent Benny had professed his feelings to her (nor was I completely convinced my friend was ready to retire his jersey as the Near West Side's number one playboy) I opted not to make a huge verbal fuss over meeting her. After all, Benny seemed effusive enough for the both of us.

"She's gorgeous isn't she?" he proclaimed, throwing all subtlety to the wind. Though I naturally agreed with him, it would have been awkward for me to vocally concur, especially in front of her sister, who clearly hadn't inherited the same exquisite features.

"And you must be Gertrude," Benny said, turning to this glum and lackluster also-ran, who looked as if she would rather be in Timbuktu. My friend threw me an apologetic sideways glance.

"That's right," the sister practically huffed. Pointing to the freshly painted walls, she added, "Why'd you miss the top part?"

"Care to explain, my acrophobic friend?" Benny asked, staring at me with a smirk.

"Come now, Nick. You're not afraid of heights?" Something about that question, or the sound of Estelle's voice as she asked it, gave me a startling sensation of déjà vu. Before I could answer, she was onto another subject. "This is so exciting, Ben!" She sized up the room with a broad smile and a glint in her eye. As she made a fuss over what we'd done with the place and how thrilled she was for us, I stared fixedly at the young woman, trying to figure out what it was that was making me feel inexplicably mesmerized by her. She was a stunner, yes, but as Benny's longtime sidekick I'd seen plenty of pretty girls. Why did this one seem so different? Perhaps I subconsciously recognized her as some sort of symbolic punctuation mark in my life. Things were bound to change between Benny and me, especially if he was truly as gone on her as he claimed. Yet that sixth sense didn't entirely account for the fact that my heart was in my throat, and I had to stop myself from staring. My train of thought was interrupted by the less-than-symphonic voice of her sister.

"You're selling pizza? That's the only thing on the menu?" Gertrude's voice failed to mask her skepticism.

"Yes, once we open in a couple of weeks, that is," I answered. Her upper lip crinkled faintly in disdain.

"From the look on your face, Gertrude, I'll take it that you've either never tasted pizza, or you've never tasted *good* pizza. I assure you, Nick and I are going to rectify that." I recognized Benny going into sales pitch mode, something we'd been rehearsing for weeks.

"I've actually never tried it, myself, to be honest," said Estelle. "You said it's like a pie, Ben? There's nothing I love more than sinking my fork into a good flaky pie crust . . . ."

"A *fork*!?" Benny threw his head back with laughter, then grabbed her hand and kissed it. "Oh, Estelle, you lovely girl. A smart cookie, but so much to learn, eh, Nick?"

"No fork," I explained to both girls. "You can eat it with your hands. And the crust isn't flaky. It's more of a perfect combination of crisp and chewy." Estelle and her sister exchanged perplexed glances.

"You eat it with your hands? Sounds positively boorish," Gertrude said.

"It *sounds* delicious," Estelle said, wrapping her arm around Benny's waist, "and I can't wait to try it." She couldn't have been more sincere in her enthusiasm. Maybe that's what had me feeling all topsy-turvy inside. The way Benny looked at her, I could tell he was besotted. But for how long? I loved him like a brother, but he'd already left a string of spurned damsels in his wake. It was statistically a near certainty that he would break this sweet and lovely young woman's heart into a thousand smithereens, like the remnants of broken glass I'd just swept up out front.

"Will you excuse us?" Gertrude said abruptly, ushering her sister by the elbow to the front of the shop. They talked in whispers, but I could tell from the look on both young women's faces that they were in disagreement with one another over something. Gertrude evidently wasn't too thrilled about being dragged into such a "boorish" establishment. Benny sidled up next to me, meanwhile, and we both watched from across the room.

"What do you think?" he asked. "Does she not have the most spectacular blue eyes you've ever seen?" My mind reeled as it hit me. Those eyes . . . the color of blue hydrangeas. Seven years had changed her, physically (and how!), and her "grown up" name had thrown me off, but it was her. *My* Stella. I hadn't recognized her at first sight, and she clearly had no inkling that we'd met before, once upon a time when she wore her hair in ponytails. Certainly Benny hadn't made the connection, nor were either of them likely to untangle our strangely entwined fates so many years after the fact. Benny had made good on his promise. He'd found her. Only this time, he was head over heels in love with her. It felt like being punched in the face all over again.

CHAPTER 7

You Kiss by the Book

THE DANCE FLOOR PROVED TO BE THE IDEAL refuge from Beresdorfer the younger, who was well on his way toward earning a new moniker: Pushy Perry. All was copacetic until I could no longer ignore the painfully obvious: my mom was trying to catch my attention from across the room. Communicating through a complicated system of vigorous hand waving (on her part) and eye rolling (on my part), we reached a détente, which was that I would spend the next hour or so "working the room," as I'd promised my dad. Like an overly ambitious gubernatorial candidate the day before an election, I kissed adorable babies, shook hands with elderly patrons, and generally played the dutiful daughter and amiable hostess. Despite the fact that I hated being on display, it was actually really touching to see that so many people had shown up for the occasion. My head spun as I interacted with an onslaught of close and distant relatives, including second and third cousins two and three times removed (whatever that meant). Mario, acting more like a furtive political aide than a maître d', shadowed me with a veritable dossier on the guests in attendance.

"That's Teresa, your cousin Dino's second wife—her first grandson was born in May."

"Teresa!" I'd chirp. "How's that baby?"

"Claire Paulinelli is over at Table Four," Mario would continue under his breath. "She sends those god-awful cookies at Christmas."

"Mrs. Paulinelli! Can I put in my order now for more of those delicious *pizzelle*?"

"They're *angeletti*!" Mario hissed, not moving his lips. He ought to consider moonlighting as a ventriloquist.

"Only kidding you, Mrs. P! Who could ever forget your *angeletti*?"

Plenty of neighbors and local business owners had shown up, and I even spied Father Vito, the pastor from Our Lady of Pompeii church, charming Carmen with his moves on the dance floor. How surreal. Most of these people, I knew, were here out of love for the restaurant and the Caputo family as a whole, and I was proud to be an extension of that unit. That being said, if I didn't get a reprieve from the fake smiling soon, I might develop a case of self-induced lockjaw.

"Hey, cuz," Ty said, coming up behind me and nudging me with his elbow, "had enough yet?"

"Yes, more than enough," I sighed. "Think you can keep my parents off my back for a few minutes while I get some air?"

"Consider it my birthday present to you," he drawled with a wink.

Moments later, true to his promise, Ty, Frankie, and Enzo launched into the clownish boy band-style dance-off they'd been performing at every family wedding since they were ten years old. Shirttails untucked and ties around their foreheads, the brothers enthusiastically karaoked their way through a cheesy pop tune, leaving no pelvic thrust or air guitar solo unturned. With guests obviously highly entertained by their antics and my parents distracted, I chose that moment to make my escape to the kitchen. I needed to sneak away for a few minutes to check in on Chef, or, truth be told, to confab with him about the mysterious guy I'd seen. The encounter, though brief, had wreaked havoc in me, body and soul. Chef would understand as no one else would. He always did. I backed into the hallway that led to the restrooms, intending to enter the kitchen from the back door when I tripped over one of a pair of preppy navy-blue deck shoes. Unfortunately, they belonged to Perry, who was blocking my potential escape route.

"Hey, I've been looking for you," he said, way too enthusiastically.

"Um, I was just on my way to . . . ." I attempted, unsuccessfully, to squeeze past him.

"I wanted to make sure we finalized plans for our date," he said, grabbing my hand with his sweaty one. Ew.

"Our *date*?" I gently tried to extricate my hand, but he held it fast. His proprietary air was really beginning to annoy me. I'd tried to be pleasant out of respect for my dad, but this was going too far. "What are you talking about?"

"If you're worried about your dad, I checked with him and he gave me his blessing." His *blessing*? I shuddered inwardly.

"Um, Perry . . . ." I backed away from him, wishing I could for once just speak my mind and tell him to go away. Instead my mom's command—"Be nice to that boy"—echoed in my brain. "I think there's been some misunderstanding—"

"Hey, *there* you are," said a voice from behind me. As though harvested straight from my (admittedly obsessed) brain, I turned and saw that it was none other than the dark-haired boy I'd noticed earlier—the very object of my idolatry. Taking my free hand, he gave Perry, who was still holding my other hand, a friendly, yet somehow dismissive, nod. I looked from one hand to the other, marveling at the strange situation I'd found myself in. "Sorry—" he started to say to Perry, and then looked at me quizzically.

"This is Perry," I said, catching on.

"And you are?" Perry asked him.

"With her," he said, winking at me and holding up our entwined hands for Perry's inspection. "As in *together*. Which means she can't go on a date with you." His tone was apologetic, but his eyes held an almost dangerous glint.

"But . . ." started Perry, confused, as he let go of my hand.

"Sorry, Barry—"

"It's Perry."

"Perry, right. See you around." Perry watched us depart, his broad, bland face expressing a mixture of irritation and perplexity. I thought we were headed for the dance floor, but still holding my hand with a confident grip, my rescuer veered in the opposite direction. He led me up the stairs to a corner of the mezzanine that had been curtained off from floor to ceiling by silver fabric to give the dance floor the feel of a stage. Behind it was the Monroe booth, which was virtually hidden from the rest of the room. He pulled aside the curtain, and we slid into the darkened nook.

Just being near him had my pulse racing, and I knew I was blushing like an idiot, which made me grateful for the lack of lighting.

"Thanks," I said. "That was getting awkward. Make that *awful*."

"No problem," he replied. My hand in his didn't feel the least bit strange. On the contrary, it felt exactly right. I waited for him to say something else, but he looked at me, calmly, as if expecting that I'd speak now.

"We haven't met before, have we?" I asked.

"Uh, no. I'm not from around here. I came with some friends. Actually," he added, "they had the idea to crash the party. I'm meeting up with them here."

"So you weren't invited?" My party had crashers? Maybe I was cooler than I thought.

"No. And, to be honest, I don't really like parties. What about you?"

"Oh, I don't usually like parties, either." Though this one wasn't turning out to be as bad as I'd imagined, I added silently to myself. Instead of responding, he nodded and smiled, waiting for me to complete my thought. I wasn't used to anyone asking for my opinion, let alone giving me the floor to say whatever it is I wanted to say, so I tentatively continued. "I mean, birthdays are fine when you're *five*," I said, "but at a certain point, get over it, right? It kind of seems redundant for every single person on Earth to celebrate their birthday once a year for the rest of their lives. A birthday once a decade after you hit ten seems like it would make more sense. Then again, I don't have much luck where birthdays are concerned, so maybe it's sour grapes."

"Do tell."

"A kid threw up on me in a birthday bounce house when I was seven. It was a pizza party, so, well . . . you can imagine. Then, when I turned ten, my mom hired a clown for my birthday. He was terrifying, and slightly drunk, and had breath so rank it could have euthanized a small animal. When I was fourteen, I had an allergic reaction to the food dye in the icing on my cake—wound up covered in hives. So you could argue that the whole 'party apathy' thing is really PTSD." I paused. Had I been rambling? If so, he didn't seem to mind. On the contrary, the devilish grin from before was back in full force and it utterly bewitched me.

"Duly noted," he finally said, nodding. "You have a wry sense of humor, do you know that?"

"Uhh, no, not really," I said. Next to my clowning cousins, I was never considered the comic relief of the family.

"Well, I like it. So if you're not into birthday bashes," he continued, "then why are you here?" He obviously had no idea who I was. It was refreshing not to have "Caputo's only daughter" stamped on my forehead, figuratively speaking.

"Oh, I work here." Which wasn't a lie.

"No kidding. I'm in food service, too."

"Waiters and waitresses get no respect," I sighed, only partly in jest.

"No doubt—those government signs in the bathroom telling us to wash our hands. Um, why is that only directed at us?"

"Right? It's ridiculous!" I laughed, feeling myself come alive. "And the crazy orders people come up with: 'I'd like a house salad,

only hold the onions, dressing, tomatoes, cucumbers, and lettuce.'
Why not just order a plate of croutons?"

"Yeah," he said. "Don't even get me started on splitting a check
nine ways."

"I can't feel too sorry for you, though. I *never* get Saturday
nights off."

"Okay, well, confession time: I'm supposed to be working,
too," he replied. "I faked a cold to get off early."

"Degenerate!"

"I know, I know. I didn't want to—come to the party, I mean.
My buddy basically badgered me into it. He thought I needed a
change of scenery and wouldn't shut up about it, so I finally gave
in. And I have to admit, it's nice to see how the other half lives for
a change."

"Agreed," I sighed. "I basically work in a windowless basement.
I swear, it's turned me claustrophobic. It can't be healthy."

"I'm right there with you. Work is like my second home, in the
best and worst sense," he noted. "What's it like working for the
Caputos, anyway?"

"You could say they're like family," I said, inwardly
congratulating myself for my artful reply.

"So, I guess you probably *had* to come to the party then?
Because of your job, I mean."

"In a manner of speaking."

"Hmmm . . . sounds like there's more you're not telling me,"
he said with a sly smile. "A sense of humor and mysterious, too—
sounds like trouble." I wondered how a stranger sitting next to me
in the dark could be more in tune with me than most everyone
else in my life. I smiled back and shrugged, partly to flirt, and
partly because telling him I was the guest of honor might be
the conversational equivalent of turning my coach back into a
pumpkin.

"Well, anyway, I'm glad," he said, more serious now.

"Glad that I was forced to attend this party against my will?" I asked with a laugh.

"No. Just glad you're here."

"Oh." There went my stomach again, as if I was slowly cresting the peak of a wooden roller coaster. My brain was a forest canopy brimming with birds—a million little thoughts I didn't know how to convey. I'd never been forthcoming with my innermost feelings, yet for some reason, I now felt a frantic need to share them with this complete stranger. The moment was strangely evanescent—as if it might vanish in an instant. I needed to keep this perfect place in time from slipping out of my grasp. But where to begin? What to say? And if I did speak, would it suddenly break the spell we both seemed to be under?

"I'm glad you're here, too," I whispered at last.

He responded, not with a word, but with a kiss. That moment I'd read about and fantasized about, but never ever actually experienced until now. Though one could argue that being a rookie precluded me from objectively describing my first romantic foray with a boy, let me only say this: If there existed some universal ledger ranking the most incomparably sublime instances of liplock in the history of all space and time, our kiss would have at least cracked the top twenty. I felt like I was falling into the most beautiful night sky I'd ever seen, filled with galaxy after galaxy of stars; an infinite series of fantastic possibilities. Everything else fell away for those few eternal moments. It was just the two of us as the whole world ceased to exist. And then it all came crashing down. Literally.

Bodies careened into our booth, and, ripped from their moorings, the curtains sheltering us from the dance floor tumbled to the floor. Just like that, the outside world came rushing back in, accompanied by sounds of outraged shouting.

"He's a Monte!" roared my cousin Ty, as he regained his balance and reached for the collar of a blond guy in a faux tuxedo T-shirt and black jeans. "Stop him!"

The boy, barely evading Ty's grasp, sprinted down the mezzanine steps and toward the front entrance of the restaurant, knocking over several bystanders who stood in his way. Frankie and Enzo had tackled someone else, and the two of them looked like they were about to start throwing punches when suddenly my father was on stage and shouting into the microphone.

"Frankie, Enzo, stop it. *Now!*" His voice was as angry as I'd ever heard it, ricocheting into the far corners of the room, every syllable punctuated by the buzz of feedback from the mic gripped tightly in his fist. Mario and Chef each grabbed a cousin by the arm, pulling them away from the interloper who stood, and, tucking in a rumpled shirt, stumbled toward the exit.

"But, Uncle Benji, don't you understand? They're Montes," Frankie said. He attempted, fruitlessly, to lunge after the departing "guests," but Chef held him fast.

"They're leaving now, see?" My father pointed toward the door where indeed the two boys had just vanished. The handsome stranger gave my hand a quick, reassuring squeeze before letting go and slipping out of our booth. My twin cousins, Enzo and Frankie, continued to argue with my father as I watched my unexpected paramour walk with what looked like effortless nonchalance to follow his friends and fellow party crashers.

"They shouldn't be here," Ty chimed in, going to stand in solidarity alongside his brothers.

"This is Gigi's party," said my dad, "and I won't let anyone ruin it. Not the Montes, and certainly not the three of you. Where *is* Gigi?" Dad craned his head around until he spotted me over his shoulder, sitting alone in the Monroe booth. Only I wasn't looking at my dad. Instead, my eyes were still trained on the first boy I'd ever kissed as he crossed the threshold of our restaurant. He turned and flashed me a heart-meltingly adorable grin. I smiled back, but as I turned away, my glance landed on my cousin Ty, who having witnessed this exchange, shouted epithets after the intruders like an angry god hurling down an ancient curse. The wooden doors of Cap's entrance slammed shut on the face I now adored, and it suddenly hit me—I didn't even know his name.

* * *

The subsequent departure of the Beresdorfers wasn't nearly as distressing to me. But maybe it should have been. Still reveling in the afterglow of my illicit liaison, I wasn't aware of this second commotion underway until I saw my parents fluttering around Perry's father, attempting to coax him into staying.

"This was trivial, really," my dad assured his new investor. "Just a couple of punk kids, but clearly no harm was done."

"I don't know, Ben, this is looking like more trouble than I initially signed up for. If you can't keep the rats away from the cheese on tonight of all nights, I'd hate to think about what other 'oversights' might occur."

"Rich, I can assure you, Cap's is a safe investment." My mother looked humiliated to have our financial dirty laundry hanging out for every guest at the party.

"I'm starting to feel like you promised me one bill of goods but sold me another," said Mr. Beresdorfer, glancing at me, for some reason.

"Not at all, Rich! Please . . . we shook hands on this."

"Sorry, Ben, but I've really got to rethink this thing."

As he and his dad said their uncomfortable goodbyes, Perry avoided eye contact with me; whether from embarrassment or anger, I couldn't be sure. Sensing the somber turn the event had taken, other party guests had begun to filter out when I felt a tap on my shoulder. It was Carmen, who whispered in my ear.

"There's a wanton shade of pink in your cheeks, my dear. Could it be from more than just dancing?"

Her insight left me momentarily speechless. Before I could respond, Mario came striding over, precise and purposeful, as always.

"If I may have a word. Your cousins are asking for you," he explained.

"And you're their emissary?"

"Your father booted them from the dining room until all the guests are gone. They're in the kitchen."

I was sure they were going to apologize for their disruptive behavior earlier, and I was ready to forgive them. I had more important things on my mind, after all. Namely, trying to figure out who in the heck it was that I'd just kissed. So what if he was friends with one of the Monte boys—or, most likely, worked at their restaurant? He could always quit. But that was assuming I'd even see him again. I couldn't believe my brain was leaping ahead to any presumptions where he was concerned. Practically speaking, my brief association with him made him only slightly more than a figment of my imagination. And yet he was consuming an inordinate amount of my brain—and my heart.

"How long have you been sneaking around with him?" Ty demanded to know when I entered the kitchen. He and his younger brothers were staring me down as if I'd just called their basketball idol, Michael Jordan, an "overrated hack."

"I haven't been 'sneaking around' with anybody. If you mean that guy I was—"

"He *means* Roman Monte," Enzo clarified. I gasped and cupped the palm of my hand over my mouth.

"Who does he think he is? Coming in here like he owns the place," Frankie mumbled angrily. "And I hope you don't think you're special to him—he's dated and discarded half the girls on this side of Taylor Street! He's just using you."

"But, I didn't . . . ." I was frankly too dumbfounded to complete my thoughts. *Roman Monte?* Holy crap. The guy of my dreams was Roman Monte?

"You *can't* and you *won't*," Ty corrected me, looking severely ticked. "Whatever is going on between the two of you—"

"Nothing's going on."

"Yeah, right," Enzo scoffed. He still had his necktie around his forehead and thus looked like a cross between a mercenary and a frat boy in training.

"Nothing's going on," Ty said pointedly, "and *nothing* ever will. Do you understand?"

"It's none of your business," I said, sulking.

"None of my business? Gigi, this is *all* of our business! This is about Cap's! This is about our family! Do you even give a damn about that?"

"Hey, ease up on her." Chef stepped forward, grabbing Ty by the shoulders, but my cousin shrugged him off, never taking his eyes off mine.

"I'm telling you, Gigi—stay away from him. If I have to talk to *him* about it, well . . . there won't be much 'talking' happening. And that will be on *you*."

"You could right-hook that slime ball into next year, T-Bone," Frankie said, urging on his big brother as if he was vying for a ringside seat.

"God," said Ty, shaking his head in disgust, "if Uncle Benji found out about this, he would go ballistic."

"He doesn't need to know," I stammered, "because there's nothing to know."

"I still say we go after them," Enzo chimed in. "Three of them, three of us? We could take 'em, easy. I'm ready to go clean some Monte clocks—how about you two?"

"The only thing you boys are cleaning up is the dining room," said Aunt Val, who'd entered the kitchen as Enzo made these threats. "Now get out there and help your aunt and uncle before I drag you all out by your ears."

The boys were cowed into submission by the only person who had any kind of real power over them: their mother. As my cousins moped their way through the swinging kitchen door, she and I followed them. My aunt tossed her arm lovingly over my shoulders.

"What a wonderful party, Gigi!" she exclaimed. "Was it everything you'd ever dreamed of?"

"Yes," I answered truthfully. And no, I thought to myself. Sure, I'd met the boy who was most likely going to haunt both my dreams and my every waking hour, but my cousins had all but promised to skin him alive if I ever saw him again. Not exactly an auspicious start to my sixteenth year.

CHAPTER 8

This But Begins the Woe
Others Must End

"HE CALLED YOU 'DIRTY DAGO SCUM?'"

"It wasn't the most favorable of introductions."

"Come on, Benny. What did you expect?"

"I didn't expect him to make me feel like a flayed side of beef."

"Yeah, well, he caught you throwing rocks at his daughter's window after midnight. You're damn lucky he didn't call the cops."

"*I* should have called the cops after the way he tried to rough me up. Why are you busting my chops about this, anyway?" I didn't answer him but just continued to unpack a crate filled with cans of imported San Marzano tomatoes, which I'd been stacking in the storeroom. In the month since our shop opened, business had been booming. The folks in this part of town might not have deemed us "white enough" to date their daughters, but they were catching on to the fact that our pizza was a small slice of heaven. Benny had been right about choosing this neighborhood. I could already see that in a few more months we'd be making money hand over fist. But I wasn't about to admit that aloud. I could barely stand to look at him. We spent thirteen-hour days together, punching and tossing the dough, ladling it with marinara, and scattering it with three fistfuls of shredded mozzarella and assorted toppings with assembly-line efficiency. Using the wooden-handled peel, we'd slide the pies from the counter into the gaping, fiery mouth of Bessie, our wood-fired oven that had been custom-built, brick by brick, to our specifications. I spent most of those hours in the kitchen steaming. Not because it was as hot as the gates of hell in front of that oven, but because I had yet to get over the fact that Benny was dating the girl who was supposed to have been meant for me.

"What's gotten into you, Nick?" Benny finally asked me, point blank.

"It's ten-thirty," I said, avoiding his question as I hauled a twenty-pound sack of flour from the stockroom and heaved it onto the counter in the kitchen. "The lunchtime crowd is going to be in soon, and we don't even have the dough mixed. Are you going to help or not?"

"Of *course* I'm going to help. Are you implying that I'm not pulling my weight around here? Because I'm pretty sure my knuckles are just as singed as yours are."

"Never mind. Just get Bessie fired up and let's get to work."

"Nicky—we're doing *good*," he said with a conciliatory smile. "This place is everything we wanted it to be. We're on our way! You really should try to enjoy that fact for a second."

"Let's not get ahead of ourselves just yet," I said, crossly.

"Hey, knock it off. You're not going to do this to us," he said, folding his arms resolutely over his chest.

"Do what?"

"Bust our balloon. Look at us, Nick! We're living the dream! We've got the business now, and I've got Estelle, and it's everything I've ever—" he stopped short when he heard my sarcastic huff. "What's your problem with Estelle?"

"I've got no problem with *Estelle*," I answered, truthfully. "She's perfect, just like you always go on and on about."

"I'm not sure I like your tone, old sport." Benny eyed me sternly. I had no intention of ever telling him that the girl of his dreams was the girl from the World's Fair. We weren't twelve years old anymore, and trying to call "firsties" on her would have demeaned all three of us. The practical side of me kept trying to tell myself that I was simply hung up on a fantasy from my childhood. I'd known her for a mere five minutes that day; she was never *mine* to begin with. It was ridiculous to feel so betrayed—Benny had no idea, after all—but my heart didn't seem to want to fall in line with the edicts of my common sense. My friend led a charmed life, and Stella was just one more example. I was sick and tired of his bread always landing buttered side up.

"If you've got something to say to me, be a man and say it," Benny ordered. The long work hours and very little sleep we'd been getting in recent months didn't augur well for the rest of this conversation.

"You just have to have it all, don't you?" My rhetorical question caused Benny's brow to furrow in confusion.

"I don't even know what that means. We split this business fifty-fifty, and if it's a girl you want—because it's starting to sound like you're jealous—then I've got news for you: Half the planet is covered with 'em. All you've got to do is go talk to one. Or do I have to do that for you, too?"

"Why not? You're good enough at it, after all," I said. "You flirt with every girl under the age of thirty who shows up at the counter, all while keeping your prized Stella on hold in case you finally decide to narrow the field to just one."

"In case? Her name's *Estelle*, and I am going to marry her, Nick. End of story. And if you think I'm flirting with our customers, well, that's all part of running a business. Just because I make eye contact with people doesn't mean I'm trying to make time with them. A little personality is all part of making a profit. You don't seem to mind when we empty out the till each night."

"I don't want to argue about this," I said, grabbing a crowbar to break down the crate I just unpacked. "You're right. We're on a roll here, and I just want to concentrate on making sure it stays that way. I hope it works out for you and your lady friend. I hope your families can somehow accept this, and the two of you can ride off into the sunset and have lots of little *bambinos* running around someday. Knowing you like I do, I'm sure it'll all work out."

Though he detected the heavy note of cynicism in my voice, Benny let it slide. He picked up a bushel of red peppers and carried it back to the front of the kitchen. I knew what the future really held for Benny and Stella: It was going to end in a broken heart. I hated to think of her getting hurt. But get too close to the sun, and you can't avoid getting burned.

Two weeks and three days later, it happened, just as I predicted. Sunday was the one day of the week Antonio's was closed, and after morning Mass at Our Lady of Pompeii, Benny took off to meet Stella for their date at the Lincoln Park Zoo. I didn't expect to see him again that day, but at three o'clock in the afternoon, as I sat on our shaded front stoop in my trousers and undershirt to cool off in the sweltering July heat, he came ambling down Taylor Street. The familiar smile that was usually plastered across his face had made itself scarce. Despite the stagnant, humid air, he had both fists shoved in his pockets and looked downright despondent as he approached. Noticing me, he startled momentarily, appearing to compose himself.

"Heya, Chief!"

"Something wrong?" I asked.

"Nah." He shook his head and shrugged, then glanced up and down the street, attempting an air of nonchalance. The leaves from the poplar tree overhead cast dappled shadows over his face.

"Where's your girlfriend? I thought you were spending the day with her?"

"It ended up being too hot and crowded at the zoo. The cages were smelling a little ripe."

"So did you go somewhere else?"

"Nah." He waved his hand as if swatting away a gnat. "Remember how hot it was that summer at the fair? It feels that hot today."

"Yeah, I guess." I agreed. "So where's Estelle?"

"I told her we needed to cool things down."

"So did you go to the lakeshore or something? Bet it was crowded *there*."

"No. I mean, I told her we needed to take a break. From each other."

A strange mix of fury and relief washed over me, but I wasn't about to let it show.

"How'd she take it?"

"She didn't say anything. There were tears. Lots of tears," he said, shaking his head and staring at the sidewalk.

"Wow, Ben. I don't know what to say. I thought you were really in love this time."

"I was." He shrugged. "It just didn't seem . . . right." I knew Benny like the back of my hand, but I couldn't get a good read on the look in his eyes. "You know me, Nick," he continued, pausing only to clear his throat. "I love garlic, but eat it for breakfast, lunch, and dinner, and I start to get a foul taste in my mouth, you know what I'm saying?" Comparing Stella to a hunk of garlic seemed callous, even for Benny.

"Time to cast the old fishing line back into the murky deep," I said, "see what else is out there?" Benny pursed his lips and shrugged again, not looking at me.

"I suppose so. Anyway, she's just a broad. No sense getting all twisted up over it. I just hope she's okay, is all." Though Stella's star had briefly shone again in my celestial orb, I expected that not even St. Anthony, patron saint of lost items, would have been able to find her again now that Benny had decided he was done with her.

* * *

For as lousy as I remained at interacting with women my own age, two-year-old Carmen seemed to think I was the bee's knees. Antonio's widow, Vera, occasionally brought the cherubic tot by the pizzeria for a visit, and I'd entertain her with sophomoric funny faces, juggling acts, and "disappearing thumb" tricks. She loved that I called her *principessa* and secretly handed her bits of pizza crust long after her mother had told her she'd had enough. One August afternoon before the dinner rush, Vera came in looking frazzled.

"Uncle Nick, she's all yours," Vera sighed, gesturing to Carmen, who stood dawdling at the doorway. "We missed the first train because she had to stop and pick dandelions."

"Come here, little lollygagger," I said, kneeling down to let Carmen leap into my arms. "You're not giving your *mammina* a rough time of it today, are you?"

"Yes, I am," the little girl proudly proclaimed.

"Get all your misbehavin' out of the way while you're still young and adorable," I teased her. "Once you're in school, the mean nuns aren't going to let you get away with it. Well, unless you're like your Uncle Benny."

"Why?"

"Because he can charm the pink off a pig."

"Why?"

"Never mind about that. Just keep on being cute is all I'm saying."

"Why?"

"Because . . . ." I glanced at Vera.

"Yes, it's incessant," she confirmed. "Like a persistent little woodpecker hammering at my soul. If you can find a way to stop it—even for a little bit—you'll have saved me from the brink of insanity."

"Oh, I think I've got an idea," I responded. I cupped my hand in front of Carmen's ear and whispered into it.

"Yes, yes, yes!" The little girl began galloping around the room.

"How about I steal this little lady for thirty minutes or so?" I asked Vera.

"Be my guest!" she responded.

"Okay," I chuckled. "Benny's in the kitchen. Tell him I'll be back before four."

Rather than stoop, hunch-shouldered, to hold Carmen's pudgy little hand out on the sidewalk, I swept her up onto my shoulders for a piggyback ride. The late summer day was pleasant, reminding me of the Irving Berlin tune "Blue Skies," which my mother always hummed on afternoons like this. A grimy-faced newsboy on the corner handed out broadsheets faster than he could collect two cents from each customer. The cover of today's *Daily Tribune* was all about the Atlantic Charter that President Roosevelt and Winston Churchill had hammered out. Everyone was desperate to know (some fearful, some hopeful) whether FDR would lead us into England's fight against Hitler and that fascist pig, Mussolini, who had brought no end of suffering to so many of our relatives back in the mother country. As an American of Italian descent, I hated the dictator, both for his Nazi alliance and for the police state Italy had become under his regime. Unfortunately, some people assumed that I and every other Italian-American tacitly supported *Il Duce,* as he was called. Anti-Italian sentiment was nothing new, but in recent years, the tone we encountered outside of our close-knit neighborhood was one of mistrust and downright hostility. The increasingly grim news coming out of Europe, coupled with the escalating tension at home, made even today's blue skies feel downright foreboding. Nevertheless, I had a two-year-old to amuse for the next thirty minutes, and there was no use dwelling on anything other than happy thoughts as I attempted to edge out Mickey Mouse on her list of favorite known entities.

"Candy! Candy! Candy!" she trilled when I finally set her back down on terra firma in front of Queenie Mab's Candy Shoppe and Soda Fountain. A leather strap of sleigh bells affixed to the door jingled as we entered the colorful shop, which smelled like a mixture of sugarplums and furniture polish. Wrought-iron chairs with heart-shaped backs flanked small wooden tables atop the black-and-white mosaic-tile flooring. Along the back wall, two soda jerks in white aprons and white paper hats scooped ice cream and mixed phosphate drinks behind an imposing oak counter. Directly in front of them—wisely marketed directly at child's-eye level—candy in egregious quantities was piled in tilted wicker baskets: peppermints and peanut butter kisses, saltwater taffy, and Snaps licorice, to name just a few.

At the cash register, pecking at the buttons with vampish red fingernails, stood Queenie Mab herself, the store's proprietress. Though I'd never seen her before, she bore an exact likeness to the cartoon drawing that accompanied her sign out front, down to the same white ruffled blouse and black pencil skirt that barely encased her bustling backside. Her graying hair was piled into a bialy-sized bun on top of her head, from which small corkscrew tendrils attempted a desperate escape.

Sizing up Carmen and me, Queenie's lips, which were painted red to match her nails, turned from a pucker to a barely perceptible sneer. Instead of taking our order, she ambled slowly to a box near the window and began counting white paper doilies. The two soda jerks a few feet away pretended not to notice us, as well.

"Excuse me," I said, to no avail.

"They don't have any *ears*," Carmen noted, more perceptively than most toddlers might.

"You're right, sweetheart," I said, perturbed, but trying not to show it. "Come on, let's pick out what we want." I ushered the little girl over to a shelf with glass jars of stick candy. As Carmen marveled over the vibrant colors spiraling like mini barber poles, I glanced back to the counter and saw that Queenie was now helping another customer. Ordinarily, I would have turned on my heel and walked out of the place, but I wasn't going to let that racist old biddy disappoint Carmen's sweet tooth.

I let the little girl pick out two sticks—one for now and one for later when Vera would need another dose of quiet serenity—and we headed back over to the counter to pay. This time, instead of ringing me up, Queenie nodded to the customer standing in line behind me.

"Can I help you, miss?" she asked, pointedly pretending not to see me.

"Yes," said the woman's voice over my left shoulder. "Three malteds, if you please. And whatever else the gentleman who's standing right in front of you is purchasing. He's with me. And he's treating."

I slowly turned around, startled by the request, and was further surprised to discover who the voice belonged to.

"Stella!" I said.

"Stella!" Carmen echoed distractedly, still staring with longing at the candy.

"Stella?" Estelle repeated the nickname with a puzzled look on her face. "Good heavens, no one's called me that since I was a little girl!"

"What are you doing here?" I wondered, rifling through my pockets for change, which I slid across the counter to Queenie.

"What any woman does when she gets thrown over by a boy," Stella replied. "Gorging myself on sugar." I smiled stupidly and cursed the fact that she'd just made it impossible to dance around the delicate topic of her and Benny's break-up. "I should be asking *you* what *you're* doing here," she continued. "Isn't half of Chicago lining up for your pizza?"

Before I could respond, she was already down on Carmen's level introducing herself. "Do you want a malted milk, my little love?" she asked. "Come with me, I can explain to you all about the dangers of spending time with handsome Italian boys." She flashed me a quick smirk, then led Carmen to a table with two chairs and pulled an empty seat from a nearby table next to it, as well. The little girl immediately began peppering Stella with questions, and as I took a seat beside them, it dawned on me that I'd suddenly become the third wheel to an impromptu ladies' luncheon. Only after Queenie delivered our tray of chocolate malteds did Carmen, kneeling on her chair to achieve enough height to reach the towering straw, stop talking.

"What a sweetheart," Stella said.

"She's a cute kid," I agreed. "She's practically family to Benny and me. I mean . . . Oh gosh, sorry."

"You can say his name," she sighed. "Oh, Nick, I just really don't know what happened." Tears started to well up in her eyes, and I prayed she wasn't about to treat me like the priest in some romantic confessional. "I'm not going to cry," she assured me, though she already had. "It's like his feelings for me changed overnight. I had absolutely no warning."

"I wish I knew what to say," I said, honestly. "If it helps at all, he really did seem to care about you."

"I thought so, too! It doesn't matter now." She dabbed the tears from her eyes with the lower end of her palm. Carmen, sipping from her straw, suddenly took notice.

"Aww, do you have a boo-boo? Let Uncle Nicky kiss it and make it better!" Stella and I exchanged timid glances, followed by awkward laughs.

"Anyway, let's talk about something else," my blushing counterpart finally said, smiling sweetly. "And call me 'Stella' again. I like the sound of it."

* * *

Three weeks later I was elbow to elbow with Benny in our restaurant's kitchen when I explained to him the good/bad news as delicately as I could.

"So you really don't mind?" I asked, nervously.

Benny stood at the prep counter, mincing an onion. With the knife in his hand and his curly hair looking comically unkempt in the heat of the kitchen, he looked apt to initiate a murder spree. Had it been any guy other than my best friend, I'd never have chosen this moment to reveal that his ex-girl and I were an item of late, and I certainly wouldn't have stood within arm's length to do it. Yet when he didn't answer right away, I took a step back, just to be on the safe side.

"You're okay with Stella and me?" I said, rephrasing the question.

"Of course I'm okay with it," he answered, wiping his eyes with the corner of his apron. "This onion. Yeesh. You take over. I need a break." He reached over and passed me the knife, and I took his spot at the counter. "Besides, I already knew," he said. He rooted around among the crates, pulled up a hothouse tomato, and began tossing it from hand to hand.

"What do you mean, you *knew*?"

"C'mon, you think I'm stupid, Nick?" He shook his head. "We've been friends since before you even cared two figs about girls." He smirked and tossed the tomato at me without warning. I caught it with both hands, and the knife clattered to the counter. "You've been floating around with that stupid grin on your face for the better part of a month," he continued. I felt myself blush to the roots of my hair. "Even a complete dunderhead would've guessed you were mooning over some doll."

"But *Stella*—I mean, Estelle?" I quickly corrected myself. "She's not just any doll."

"Stella. I like that," he said, appearing thoughtful. "It suits her. And I should know more than anyone that she isn't just any doll. But," he added quickly, "if you're worried that I'm upset because I'm . . . because I dated her, then stop worrying, kid. It's water under the bridge. The past is the past, all that stuff."

"Are you sure, Benny?" I said. "Because it's important to me that you're okay with this." This was true, but only up to a point. With or without Benny's blessing, now that I had Stella, I knew I would never let her go. I was on cloud nine, but it could be a definite ten or eleven if I knew with absolute certainty that Benny could be happy for us.

"Okay with it? I'm thrilled for you." He made a move as if to punch me in the shoulder. I evaded him, and his fist hung in the air for a few seconds, targetless. "But don't think that means I'm okay with you ditching your duties here to spend time with her."

"Of course not!"

"Good, because we can't afford to slow down one iota. No resting on our laurels. Everything we've worked for—"

"I know. I know." I put my hand on his shoulder, looking him in the eye so he'd know I was serious. "You can count on me. This place is my dream as much as it is yours, and we'll always be in it together. I won't let you down."

"I believe you, Nick. Know why?"

"Why?"

"Because if you did, I'd give you a knuckle sandwich, like I did when we were kids." He shook his fist with a laugh as he said this. I remembered the shiner he'd given me that fateful day, the day I'd met Stella. I wondered for a second if he knew more than he was letting on, that Estelle and Stella were one and the same. Nah. He wasn't that good a liar.

CHAPTER 9

My Only Love Sprung from My Only Hate

JUST AS I FEARED, having changed from my party dress back into my tank top and cutoffs, I felt tragically Cinderella-like, wet-mopping what had been the dance floor. It was after midnight. I was no longer the birthday girl, so I didn't presume to exempt myself from clean-up duty. Besides, given the hardened looks on my parents' faces, it seemed unwise to be anything other than the obedient daughter. Mr. Beresdorfer's parting remarks had cast a pall over the entire evening's events, and though I was pretty sure my dad had been too distracted to notice me consorting with "the enemy," for lack of a better term, it was all I could think about. What sort of girl kisses a boy without even knowing his name? Had that really been *me*? It all seemed so surreal. Stranger still, there was no telling if—or how—I would ever see him again. He was *Roman Monte*, after all. I still hadn't fully digested that piece of information. As I mopped to the rhythm of these inner musings, Enzo and Frankie stripped the white linens off tables and replaced them with our traditional checkered tablecloths. Over at the dessert table, Mom and Aunt Val put plastic wrap over what little remained of the tiramisu, *torta della nonna*, and rum cake.

"Do you think Rich meant it?" I heard my aunt whisper under her breath to Mom.

"I don't know. This is our worst fear realized. Ben is beside himself."

"I'm so sorry the boys reacted the way they did, Nora. Where the Montes are concerned, they get a little trigger-happy." My mom sighed, shaking her head as she collected the pie servers in her hand.

"Actually . . . I suspect this may be more about Rich's son . . . and Gigi."

I wanted to interrupt them, to somehow defend myself, but it was hard to find the words. Intuitively, I knew my encounter with Perry and Roman had triggered this debacle, and yet I had no regrets. Apologizing for what had happened would have been like seeking forgiveness for having blue eyes or begging someone's pardon for having the audacity to breathe. The phrase "falling in love" suddenly made perfect sense to me. I hadn't chosen it—I'd simply stumbled over a precipice, into a sublime chasm from which I knew there'd be no climbing back out (as if I would ever want to). Even still, replaying in my head my all-too-brief conversation with Roman—and that kiss—sent aftershocks through the surface of my skin, like seismic shivers. It had all transpired the way a dream unfolds, as if the universe had somehow decreed it. His name, at the time, had been entirely beside the point, inconsequential. Now I realized that the universe had only been playing a sick joke on me.

Across the room, Ty descended a stepladder. He chucked the balled-up curtains that had been part of the decor into a cardboard box in the corner, then carried the ladder to the stairwell out back, shooting me a furtive scowl as he passed. His brow was still furrowed—though a bit less severely—when he reemerged in the dining room. As I watched him stack the chafing dishes and Sterno cans on the buffet table, I told myself that he'd be over it soon. Sure, he held grudges with a white-knuckled grip, but never with me, his favorite.

I ordinarily would have wheedled Ty into emptying my dirty mop water, but I dared not try my luck tonight. Instead, I propped the mop against a table and hoisted the heavy plastic bucket by its flimsy wire handle. I shuffled carefully to the back door, sliding my flip-flops in short steps and bending my torso as a counterbalance to keep the gray sudsy water from sloshing over the sides of the pail.

Outside, hemmed in by brick walls and a steep flight of stairs that led up to the alley, I carefully poured the contents of the bucket down the drain in the back stairwell's concrete floor. When the bucket was empty, I inhaled deeply, faintly registering the "orchard apple" scent of my drugstore shampoo and conditioner. (Inside, the restaurant always smelled like a mixture of garlic, candle flame, and Chianti.) The night air felt cool and refreshing here in this small, dank space, and I felt the goose bumps on my upper arms almost jump off my skin. Not wanting to go back inside and face my relatives again just yet, I closed the back door and leaned against it, simultaneously pulling my phone out of my back pocket. I needed to tell someone about my encounter with Roman and figured Bethany wouldn't mind if I called her this late. Her voicemail picked up instead.

"Hey, Bethany—it's me. Sorry the party ended on such a weird note after everything just—well, you know. When you get this message, call me back. I met a guy. The most amazing guy I've ever laid eyes on. I think I'm in—" *Beep!* Shoot. Her voicemail had cut me off.

"You think you're in what?" Like a nightingale, the voice fluttered in the alley somewhere above my head. I peered up the stairwell and instinctively reached for the door handle.

"Who's there?" I called out.

"For the record, I think you're amazing, too. Not to mention beautiful." He leaned over the brick wall at the top of the stairs, his face illuminated by the motion sensor light that shone from above him. He hadn't left after all, and he'd overheard my confession, too. I would have been more embarrassed had I not been so completely disarmed by his frank, self-assured response.

"What are you doing here?" I asked, trying to hide my confusion. Without thinking, I started to walk up the staircase toward him, but then Ty's warnings began clanging like a cathedral bell in my brain. What did I *really* know about him, other than that he was a sworn enemy? I hesitated on the third step, my heart willing me to climb higher, my head warning me to be cautious.

"I'm not the sort of guy who would ditch a girl without saying goodbye," he answered, "even if all her relatives want my head on a stake. I'm Roman, by the way."

"Yeah, I figured *that* one out. I'm Gigi. Well . . . technically, my name is Julietta, but everyone calls me Gigi. You know, if anyone finds you here . . . ."

"I don't scare that easily," he said, beckoning me with an outstretched arm. "Besides, I'm pretty sure you're worth the risk."

The thought of anyone hurting him made me feel strangely, fiercely protective. I took another step toward him and paused, hovering between two warring desires. Succumbing to Roman's gravitational pull would undoubtedly cause a deep rift with my family. But, as much as they wanted to, neither my cousins nor my parents had any real right to dictate who I could and couldn't be with. After all, this wasn't the sixteenth century. And what had being a "good girl" gotten me so far? With that thought, for the moment at least, my heart won a swift and decisive victory over my head. I bolted up the stairs, and he grabbed my hand, the momentum of which sent me colliding into his chest.

"Wait. Come with me," I said, leading him down the alley until we turned the corner onto a side street. He pulled me closer, and then suddenly our kiss from earlier that evening continued, as though our previous encounter hadn't been unceremoniously interrupted. The warmth of his hand cradling my neck made my pulse quicken, and it took sheer will to stop for a breath of air. When I did, I felt dizzy.

"I didn't know you were a—" he started.

"I can't believe you're a—" I said at the same instant. We both burst into spontaneous laughter, and I felt as bubbly as a bottle of Pellegrino before remembering that we were facing a very real problem.

"But seriously," I said, unable to temper my smile, "I'm sort of supposed to hate you."

"Likewise. But I've never been the type to do something just because I'm supposed to. And besides, I couldn't hate you if I tried." He reached down and tucked a stray hair behind my ear. "So what are we going to do about it?"

"I don't know," I said with a sigh. "God, this isn't very practical."

"You sound just like my great-granddad."

"I'm not sure how to take that," I said, laughing. "As long as I don't *look* like him, I guess?"

"*Hardly*. He's ninety-three years old and has eyebrows like garden hedges. *Total* curmudgeon. You, on the other hand . . . I've never seen anyone more beautiful."

I blushed, grazing his cheek with my thumb and feeling the unyielding line of his cheekbone. He placed his hands on my hips, and my knees almost buckled. This was happening. *Again.* Inside, I felt a crazy combination of fragility and strength. I was frightened by the intensity of my feelings. Could I trust them; could I trust him? As if perceiving the direction my thoughts had veered, Roman silenced them with another kiss.

"Of all people," I finally said, trying to keep a hold of my senses, "why do you have to be Roman Monte? Why couldn't you just be 'Joe Schmo?'"

"I'd change my name if I could. Only it wouldn't change the situation. Montes and Caputos are like . . . I don't know . . . toothpaste and orange juice. Each fine on their own merits, but not meant to intermingle."

"That's putting it mildly. But it seems like our families should have everything in common. So why all the bad blood?" He shrugged and lowered his forehead to lean it against mine.

"I don't know. Looking at you, I just can't fathom how—" Unduly tempted by the close proximity of his lips to mine, I interrupted him with another kiss. We were too swept up in the moment to hear the footsteps approaching, and were only startled apart by the sound of the lid opening on a nearby dumpster. About twenty yards away stood Chef, giant white garbage bags hanging from each fist.

"Cap's dumpsters are full," he informed me, seemingly unfazed at having caught me mid-makeout. "Your mother is wondering where you are. You should come back inside."

"Okay. Just give me a minute." Chef eyed me askance, but I responded by silently imploring him, *Cover for me. I'll be right there!* Without a word, he tossed the garbage bags into the dumpster, banged the lid shut, and headed back toward Cap's. When he was out of sight, Roman took my hands again, intertwining my fingers in his.

"Will he be returning with an angry, pitchfork-wielding mob?" he asked, nodding in the direction Chef had gone.

"No, he's cool. But I should go. Things went from bad to worse after you left the party, and . . . well, it doesn't matter."

"When can I see you again?" Roman asked.

"Tomorrow afternoon?" I suggested. He reached into the back pocket of my cutoffs, grabbed my phone, and proceeded to input a string of numbers. A clanging guitar tune began emanating from his own phone but stopped after the second ring. He slid my phone back.

"Now I have your number. I'll text you when and where we can meet."

He put both hands gently behind my neck and pulled me in for one final kiss.

"I've got to go," I finally said, reluctantly breaking away from him. I made it about halfway down the alleyway when I heard him call my name.

"Gigi! Wait!" He jogged over and stopped short, breathing hard.

"What is it?"

"I'm not sure." He stared absently at a mostly-deserted parking lot as if grasping for elusive words before returning his gaze to me. "I guess I just wanted to say that who you are doesn't change anything for me."

"I feel the same way."

"Then we'll figure it out."

"Okay," I half-whispered, the night breeze dancing across my face. The moment felt almost too intense. "We'll find a way to make them understand." *Or die trying,* I told myself, remembering that my family and/or his might kill us for this.

Descending the stairs to Cap's back door, it occurred to me that my mind was gone, abandoned in some cosmic lost and found box—the place where sanity ends up after it flies out the window. This was crazy. And I didn't care. My party had ended on a sour note, but surely my parents were overreacting about that whole blow-up with Mr. Beresdorfer. Adults always seemed to accuse teenagers of acting like everything was life or death, yet it was surprising how often they did the same thing. As for the situation with Roman, it was admittedly tricky. But why couldn't this be an opportunity to establish some sort of détente between our families?

I suggested as much to Chef about thirty minutes later. Urgently needing to vocalize the conflicted thoughts racing through my brain, I had offered to stay behind with him to help prep pizza dough for the next day. (Overnight fermentation of the yeast was the secret to Cap's perfect crust.) Assured that I'd hitch a ride home with him once we'd finished up, my weary parents left through the front door, hauling a cardboard box containing unopened birthday gifts from various guests. Aunt Val and my cousins had already taken off, too, leaving me a chance to confide in the one person who always allowed me to speak my mind without an obligatory lecture factoring in.

"And you don't think he and his goombas might have actually come here tonight trolling for trouble? That's what Ty seems to think," Chef commented after I ran through the details of my new romantic entanglement. I shook my head from my perch atop the bar stool that I'd dragged into the kitchen.

"Roman had no idea who I was. I'm sure of that. He's nothing like what everyone here seems to think."

"He's got a face, I'll grant him that," Chef said. He flipped a switch on our industrial-sized electric mixer, and the dough hook began to pummel a wet mixture of flour, salt, ice water, olive oil, and yeast into a sticky mass. The machine's noise made it momentarily too loud to continue our conversation. Tapping his watch and smiling at me, Chef plucked a sprig of rosemary from a glass by the sink and handed it to me. I lifted the small branch to my nose and inhaled deeply. Eventually turning off the mixer, Chef used both hands to haul the dough onto the flour-sprinkled surface of the counter.

"Promise me you won't tell my parents," I pleaded with him, resuming our discussion.

"Oh, *bella mia*," he sighed and shook his head, beginning to cut the dough into smaller portions using a blade-like metal scraper. "I don't feel right about keeping things from your parents."

"Please—just for a little while, until Roman and I can figure out some sort of game plan." Chef looked at me with a resigned expression.

"I won't say anything . . . for now. But who's to say Ty won't?"

"He's furious with me," I conceded. "And even more furious with Roman."

"He's worried about you. And I can't say that I don't have some misgivings about this myself. Your families are at war."

"For no good reason."

"I wasn't aware that kissing a boy could cause amnesia. Need I remind you that the Montes have put us underwater in more ways than one?"

"I haven't forgotten any of that. That's what I'm trying to end. This back and forth tit for tat has got to stop sometime. The fact that nobody can even explain what first started the animosity is ludicrous. And now, because a bunch of stupid people had to do stupid things to each other, Roman and I have to sneak around like criminals." My voice started to crack as I spoke, and I felt hot tears well up in my eyes.

"Oh, Bird," Chef said, stroking my shoulder. "I know how profound this all feels, and I won't for one second make light of what you're going through. But you're exhausted. A good night's sleep will do you good."

"It's only that I finally found someone who truly gets me—besides you, of course. I know how crazy this sounds," I said, sniffling, "but even though we've only known each other for a few hours, it's like we're meant for each other."

"It doesn't seem crazy, Ladybird. It's just that—"

"Up until now, I've always followed the rules," I said, interrupting him. "Can't I have a say in my life, just this once?"

"Don't cry, sweetheart. I hate not being able to fix this for you. But—" He drummed his floury fingers on the counter. "—I think I know someone who might be able to help."

CHAPTER 10

The Earth Hath Swallow'd
All My Hopes But She

"SORRY, MISTER!"

A small boy, all elbows and knees, bolted past me wearing an elaborate feathered headdress that had slipped down over one eye. Following him were two even smaller cohorts, both of whom wore black construction paper Pilgrim hats. I grinned, remembering how Benny and I used to roam the busy sidewalks with similar abandon every Columbus Day. This beautiful, balmy October day couldn't have been any more made to order for the community's annual salute to the venerated Italian-born explorer. After dusting off the now scuffed toe of one of my newly shined shoes, I straightened up to survey the throng of revelers that swirled around me like confetti. Most lined the route of the parade as it flowed up Taylor Street, the hub of our city's Italian-American community. I was headed downstream to meet Stella.

Pulling my pocket watch from my vest, I checked the time, then, out of habit, ran my hand over the engraved initials on the back. The watch had belonged to my father, and to my grandfather before that. The fact that my mother was meeting Stella for the first time today made me wish Pops could have been around to meet her, too. Stella . . . I can't tell you how many times I'd pinched myself since that day at Queenie's. Things had just clicked between us in a way that felt almost preordained.

It was as if fate had been hatching a plan all this time to bring us back together (notwithstanding kismet's accidental detour with Benny—but hey, not even destiny can be expected to bat a thousand). I peered through the crowd. Floral replicas of the *Niña*, the *Pinta*, and the *Santa María* floated past in the shadow of a benevolent brick sphinx, Our Lady of Pompeii. Although requisite Italian flags flew as far as the eye could see, far more people brandished the good old red, white, and blue. American pride trumped all.

"Nick! Over here!" I turned my head to see Stella waving at me. After threading our way through the crowd to one another, she raised up on the balls of her feet to kiss me, which always had the effect of making my inner Clark Kent feel as if taking flight might actually be doable.

"Hi there," I said, putting her arm through mine. "Nervous?"

"A little," she replied, "but you swore she won't bite, so I guess it won't be so bad."

"It will be fine," I promised, pulling her closer, "as long as you're hungry."

"Am I ever! I didn't eat a thing this morning, on purpose."

"Good, because that's the only thing that might turn her against you: a lack of appetite for her cooking." Stella laughed, but I noticed her brow furrow slightly. "Don't worry," I added. "I'm only joking. She'll adore you, just like I do."

"Well, the way you miraculously charmed my father the other day, I guess it's only fair that I run the gauntlet, too," she said. It was true—I had expected Stella's old man to have marshaled me out of his parlor with a rifle after the way Benny had described him, but at our recent introduction, he'd been guardedly civil, if not congenial. As nervous and deferential as I'd been, her father must have viewed me as a marked improvement over Benny, a.k.a. "Mr. Smiles and Swagger." I can't imagine Stella's parents were exactly thrilled that their daughter was dating an Italian, but they'd probably long since come to terms with what I was just beginning to understand: Stella was strong-willed and not liable to be talked out of anything.

"Your Pops? He's an overgrown teddy bear," I reflected. "It's your sister who *really* scares the bejeezus out of me."

Stella placed her hands on her hips in mock reproach, but her grin ceded my point.

A few hours later, Carmen was curled up contentedly in Stella's lap, her head crowned with haphazardly pinned "Injun feathers," and her chubby hand gripping a spoon with the last vestiges of gelato still clinging to it.

My mother smiled down at us from one end of the communal table that had been set up in front of our apartment building, where she was refilling old Mrs. Garcetti's jelly-jar glass with homemade wine. The table had been piled high with plates of pasta, sardines, and other specialties lovingly prepared by the neighborhood matriarchs, but now that everyone and their twelfth cousin had committed that quintessentially Italian sin of gluttony, the remaining food would be sent over to the parish charity.

"I told you she'd love you," I whispered in Stella's ear, nodding toward my mother. Ma's friendly and welcoming demeanor had surprised even me, considering that, until this day, she'd rudely referred to Stella as a "medigan"—a slang put-down referring to the fact that she wasn't Italian. But upon meeting my shining star and seeing how happy she made me, Mother's reservations vanished almost as quickly as her world famous cannoli.

A few yards away, Benny was playing catch with two of his younger brothers, but their diversion was cut short when the ball bounced off a plate of Mrs. Lombardi's leftovers.

"Game called on account of meatballs," Benny teased the kids, tossing his glove onto the table.

"Meatballs!" trilled Carmen.

"Careful, little one," said Benny coming up from behind us and scooping up the little girl from her enviable nest. "You'll get ice cream on Stella's dress."

"Stella doesn't mind," said Carmen.

"She minds. She's just too nice to tell you so." He set her down and patted her head. "Run along now, little chief. Go help your mama clear the table."

"Hello, Ben," said Stella, standing up to face him. "How are you?"

"Hey, kid," he said, reaching out his hand to shake hers. "No hard feelings, right?" Stella gave him her hand.

"Of course not. It's funny how things have a way of working out the way they're always meant to." She shot me one of her spine-tingling grins. "I hope we can all be friends."

"Sure, sure," he said, as if trying to change the subject. "Nicky tells me you two are going to the community dance tonight?"

"Yes, that's right."

"Great," he said, turning to me. "Maybe we can go as a double date, then?"

I already knew that Benny had offered to take Carmen's mother, Vera, to the dance—a thoughtful gesture considering the twenty-seven-year-old widow rarely got the opportunity to let her hair down any more. (I had ribbed my cohort earlier this morning about the fact that he was now only four dames away from dating his way to the letter Z.) Though I, of course, knew Benny's feelings for Vera were strictly platonic, Stella was none the wiser.

"Sure, Benny," I replied. "I mean, if that's okay with Stella?" I glanced at my girl to gauge her reaction for any indication she might still be carrying a torch, no matter how small, for Benny. Would the thought of him with another woman elicit any green-eyed monsters?

"Why, of course—that's a brilliant idea!" she said. The earnestness of her smile as she entwined her arm around my waist laid all of my lingering doubts to rest. Any feelings Stella had formerly held for Benny were—just like his—buried in the past.

"So, what do you think of Vera?" I asked Stella a few hours later as we stood on the edge of the VFW Hall's "dance floor." I handed her a paper cup filled with red punch. She looked up at the ceiling as though hoping to find the answer festooned along with the paper streamers that lightly swayed each time the doors at the end of the room opened from the outside.

"Oh, she's lovely," she said, taking a sip of her punch as she tapped one foot to the music, "although she's . . . not at all what I expected."

"You don't sound convinced," I teased.

"Well, I don't know. I just thought she'd be more . . . ."

"More like you?"

"No. Well, maybe. I mean, people have types, don't they?"

"I think it's fair to say that *every* girl is Benny's type," I said. Watching the dance floor where he and Vera boogie-woogied to Count Basie, I turned my gaze back to Stella. Had I been wrong to assume that a part of her heart didn't still belong to Benny? "In case you're wondering," I continued, "*I* do have a very specific type."

"Is that right?" Stella said, coyly.

"Yes. Can you guess what it is?"

"Oh, I hate guessing games." Her eyes sparkled with mischief. "Just tell me."

"Sharp as a tack, blonde hair, hydrangea-blue eyes, and, oh . . ." I put my hand level with the top of her head. " . . . about this tall."

"Oh, Nick!" She giggled and placed her cup on the table behind us before grabbing my hand. "Let's dance."

As we swayed on the dance floor to a slow tune, I held her close. Praying she felt as lucky to be in my arms as I did in hers, I whispered into her ear: "I mean it, Stella. You're my type. Just you."

"Lucky for you, I'm all yours," she replied.

* * *

"Next stop, Halstead Street!" called out the conductor. I was standing at the back of an 'L' train car, one hand gripping the leather strap that hung from the ceiling; with the other, I nervously checked the inside pocket of my wool coat.

"You need to eighty-six that," Benny said for my ears only, his gloved hand cupped around his mouth. "If there's a pickpocket on this train, he's already marked you a few stops back."

"What?" I feigned innocence.

"You couldn't be more obvious if you were flashing that ring on your pinkie like Bugsy Siegel."

"All right. Point taken." I fought the urge to pat the outside of my jacket.

"Just doing my job," he said, barely restraining a smirk.

"Are you my best man, or my babysitter?"

"I won't be either if you chicken out. Bawk-bawk."

"Not a chance. Whether the answer is yea or nay, I'm asking her tomorrow night."

The train lurched to a stop, and the doors slid open. As we stepped out of the car and onto the platform, I lifted my coat collar around my ears to block the gusty winds. Chicago in December really knew how to test your mettle. Yet despite the bleak, thirty-degree day, my heart felt warm and downright sunny as I imagined my future state of marital bliss with Stella. Assuming she answered correctly, that is.

"Don't worry, pal," Benny said, reading my mind. "She'll say yes."

The following afternoon, Benny grumbled as he lay on his back under the sink in our pizzeria's kitchen. "If you think these old pipes are bad now, just wait till they freeze over this winter," he sighed.

"Hell will freeze over before the pipes do," I reassured him, handing a wrench down to him while dressed in my finest tweed suit.

"Since when did you become the eternal optimist? Oh, never mind, I think I know. Hey turn up the box, will ya?" Benny said, referring to the radio program *Spirit of '41*.

"You missed the end under all that banging you were doing," I answered. "*The World Today*'s about to start."

"I could tell them a thing or two about the world today," he huffed. Granted, the news overseas was getting more disturbing by the day, but my usually jovial friend was crankier lately than I'd ever known him to be. Maybe the situation in Europe was worrying him more than I realized, but I suspected his problems might lie closer to home. I chose not to nag him for answers, figuring he'd talk when he was ready. Or maybe it was just that, on some level, I didn't really want to know what was bothering him. It was my turn to be happy, damn it. My heart did somersaults in anticipation of my momentous afternoon with Stella.

The thirty-second advertising jingle concluded with a flourish, and then, rather than the opening of *The World Today*, the radio crackled as though broadcasting a particularly violent thunderstorm.

"The Japanese have attacked Pearl Harbor by air, President Roosevelt has just announced," a somber voice relayed in a tone filled with portent. Then silence.

"What was that?" Benny said, sitting up from under the sink. "*Pearl Harbor?*"

"Just a second." I ran over and twisted the knob to another station. A few more seconds of distorted crackling, then: " . . . It's no joke; it's a real war."

The bell on the front door of the shop jingled, and high-heeled shoes clicked across the tiled floor toward the kitchen.

"Nick?" Stella's voice rang out, her voice cheerful. "Am I too early?" I was suddenly despondent.

"No, Stella," I said, walking over to her and taking her hands in mine. "You're too late."

CHAPTER 11

Here's Much to Do with Hate, But More with Love

WHEN I AWOKE THE MORNING AFTER my sweet sixteen party, the hot summer sun had already laid brazen claim to my tiny bedroom under the eaves of our house. The day was going to be a scorcher. I drowsily rolled over and glanced at the time on my phone: twenty minutes to eleven. Roman and I had texted each other well into the night, and even when we'd finally agreed to turn in, the mere thought of him kept me awake for what seemed like hours beyond that. Though I'd clocked only five hours of sleep, at best, it didn't take much to return to the land of the living—remembering him brought me to in an instant.

He and I had agreed to meet at Arrigo Park at noon, which left me only about an hour to get ready. After shimmying into my favorite cotton sundress and primping for considerably longer than I normally would have, I made my way downstairs and poured a cup of the stale coffee my parents had brewed hours ago. Nuking it in the microwave for twenty seconds to reheat, I grabbed three small *pignoli* cookies from the white cardboard bakery box on the counter and popped the first one into my mouth. I thought about my agenda for later in the day and wondered if Chef's suggestion from last night would be the first step toward brokering a peace between my family and Roman's. My head said "unlikely," but my heart thought "maybe." Retrieving the mug of reheated coffee, I joined Mom and Dad at the dining room table where they sat in front of a pile of accounting books and paperwork. Neither one of them glanced up or relaxed their furrowed brows when I took a seat.

"Morning," I ventured, my voice still gravelly.

"Barely," said my father while eyeing a spreadsheet. For a brief moment, I thought he was on my case again for sleeping late. As it happened, he was on another train of thought altogether. "We've *barely* got enough to pay our suppliers next month as it is—that's assuming business returns to what it was before we were shuttered. I was depending on that reserve from Rich's loan to give us a cushion for the next few months until we're back in the swing of things."

"We've already spent most of the loan on the cleanup and renovation," my mom pointed out. "How can he just demand we repay it all immediately? I thought you and he signed some sort of contract."

"Yeah. One *he* drew up." Dad tossed a packet of legal-sized paper across the table to land in front of my mother, then reached over and pointed to one line in particular, one I could only suspect made Perry's dad God and gave my own dad zero recourse to do anything about it. "Damn it all to hell!" Dad yelled, beginning to reveal his normally latent Sicilian temper. "Pops drilled it into my head over and over for as long as I can remember: 'Don't do business with friends.' Now I know why, only it's too late to do a damn thing about it!"

"Mom?" I interrupted, searchingly. My mother held up her hand to silence me, still addressing my dad.

"What *exactly* did Rich say when he called here this morning? I just don't understand why he's suddenly reversing course on this. Last night was hardly a 'fiasco,' as he put it."

"I wish I knew, Nora. The bigger question now is, how are we going to pay him back his money and pull ourselves out of this mess?"

"Perry's dad wants the loan repaid? Already?" I asked. I put my hand to my stomach as it churned in protest. Black coffee and cookies hadn't been a good idea. My question floated in the ether, unanswered.

"If it's a matter of payroll, Ben, you know everyone at Cap's would understand if we needed to institute a temporary pay cut."

"*What's* going *on?*" I repeated, wondering why they always seemed to have selective hearing where I was concerned. How (and why) Rich Beresdorfer had reneged on his loan to my father remained unclear to me, but my parents' obvious distress said everything I really needed to know. The situation was far more serious than I had realized.

"If only it were as simple as pay cuts," continued my father. "It's going to take a lot more money to close the gap. I've been poring through these books all morning and can't seem to come up with any sort of solution other than—" My dad glanced at me, then at my mother, who placed her palm to her forehead as if soothing a migraine.

"She really ought to be told, Ben," she said with a note of defeat. "We'll have to tell her soon enough."

"Tell me what?" I gripped the sides of the upholstered dining room chair I was sitting on, as if the whole thing was about to lurch forward.

"Dad's cousin Jimmy in Peoria has a vacant property down there. The rent is almost half of what we're paying on Taylor Street," explained Mom.

"So?" Now was hardly the time for them to consider letting some random relative start up a franchise, but watching my parents exchange hesitant glances, it suddenly dawned on me: That's not what they were getting at—at all.

"You'd move Cap's? Out of Chicago?" I felt the blood drain from my face. More than three generations of Caputos had run the family business in its Taylor Street location. It was iconic. An institution. Uprooting the restaurant would be akin to pulling the plug on over half a century's worth of family history—and damn near a century's worth of of *Chicago* history. And *Peoria?* It was almost three hours away. If the restaurant moved there, it'd mean we'd be moving, too. I'd rather die, first. A million protestations were formulating in my brain, but before I could give them utterance, my dad reached across the table and gripped my shoulder.

"Nothing's settled, Gigi," he attempted to reassure me. "I'm going to go down and talk to the bank tomorrow, so this may all right itself yet."

"And we're not going to mention this to anyone—for now," added my mom. Without a word, I rose and walked out of the room, my eyes burning with the promise of impending tears. Less than a minute later, I passed back through the dining room wearing sunglasses and my purse slung over one shoulder.

"Where are you off to, Gigi?" Mom asked. Given my parents' current preoccupation, I honestly hadn't predicted this question. My brain scavenged for a plausible piece of fiction.

"To meet Bethany," I answered, as casually as I could muster in my now worked-up state. "She wants to go thrift shopping in Bucktown." Given the offhand lie, black coffee on an empty stomach, the anticipation of seeing Roman again, and now, my family's grimly uncertain future—is it any wonder my hand visibly trembled on the metal handle of the front screen door as I latched it closed?

* * *

I was a snotty, red-faced, puffy-eyed mess by the time I arrived at the park to meet Roman. He was already waiting at our agreed-upon rendezvous spot near the statue of Christopher Columbus, leaning insouciantly against the fence that surrounded the looming bronze figure and its accompanying fountain. His charming grin gave way to concern as I approached.

"What's the matter?" he asked. I said nothing, but practically collapsed against his chest, the tight pain in my lungs finally dissolving into sobs. He held me tight, occasionally stroking my hair, but not saying another word until I finally pulled back to face him.

"I'm *so* sor-sor-sorry," I stammered. "I feel so stupid."

"Tell me. I'm listening," he said. I started to explain, in short bursts between hiccups and tears, about the financial trouble besieging my parents.

"My dad says we . . . we might have to *move*," I sobbed. "Uproot the restaurant, our family—everything." The park was crowded, and people walking by couldn't help but stare at me, the personified train wreck. I felt like a complete freak show.

"What did *you* say?" Roman asked.

"Nothing," I replied. "What could I say? It's not up to me."

A little boy tossing pennies in the fountain began offering a play-by-play commentary on my own waterworks display.

"Mommy, Daddy—that girl is *crying*," he proclaimed, pointing a stubby finger in my direction.

"Come with me," said Roman as I tried to avoid the overt stares of all the other lookie lous. "I know somewhere we can be alone."

It goes without saying that I had never before seen the inside of Monte's. So when we arrived on enemy turf, curiosity helped suppress some of my earlier anguish. That, plus the fact that I was willing every nerve in my body not to fall apart again in front of Roman.

"Nobody comes in until around two-thirty to start prepping for dinner," he assured me, unlocking a side entrance. I crept lightly across the red tile floor, feeling almost as if I was trespassing—a cat burglar mid-heist or a school kid sneaking into a church sacristy to steal the communion wine. The dining room was deserted and quiet. Wooden chairs were overturned on the tables, and even with very little light filtering through the stained glass windows, I could still see the trademark touches of a traditional Italian eatery. Decor-wise, the place didn't look all *that* different from Cap's, notwithstanding the faux Tuscan wall mural which was framed by painted grape leaves and cherubs who looked like they'd eaten one too many servings of baked ziti.

"Are you hungry?" Roman asked, leading me into the kitchen. "They say there's nothing so terrible a full stomach can't start to fix. I can make you something, if eating here doesn't amount to treason for you."

"I'm pretty sure it does," I said. "But I'm famished. I didn't get to eat anything at the party, and all I had this morning were a few cookies."

"You need some protein," he said, before opening the industrial-sized fridge and removing a carton of eggs. "How about a frittata?"

"You cook?"

"I'm *Italian*. What kind of question is that?" He drizzled olive oil in a pan on the stove while I leaned against the counter opposite to watch. "Of course, you'll be the judge of whether I can compete with you. Mushrooms?"

"Sure," I said. He removed a white towel that was covering a plastic bin of earthy brown morels and began chopping them on a cutting board. "I wouldn't worry," I added, "about competing with me, I mean."

"Oh, so you're *that* good in the kitchen?"

"Hardly."

"You can't cook?" He dropped a handful of the mushrooms into the hot skillet. The hiss of the oil sounded like it was scolding me for my lack of culinary acumen.

"Oh, I can go through the motions, help around the kitchen and all that," I explained, hoping my honesty wasn't going to earn me a check in his "'cons'" column. "But if the secret ingredient of all food is love, well, I'm sort of missing that part. It's just not my passion."

"Fair enough," he shrugged, beginning to crack eggs into a stainless steel bowl. "So what is your passion? You don't seem like the type to be gunning for a spot as the next American pop diva." He reached for a whisk from a canister of cooking implements.

"Heck, no. I sing worse than I cook," I assured him. "I'm not exactly sure what I want to do. I'm supposed to run Cap's someday, I guess."

"I'm blown away by your enthusiasm," he said, tossing a large wooden pepper mill from one hand to the other before grinding it over his bowl. "I mean, running this restaurant would be my dream job."

"Not me." I shook my head. "Of course, it might not even matter, now. God," I said, staring down forlornly at my dingy white sneakers. "I've always dreaded the idea of having to take over the business some day, but now I feel so guilty—like I willed this to happen, or something."

A moment of awkward silence passed before I finally worked up the nerve to raise the question I really wanted answered. Cap's wasn't in a downward spiral for no good reason. My family had been led down this road to ruin by an outside, hostile force. I needed to know before this . . . *whatever* it was with him went any further. "Do you know anything about our fire alarm getting set off a few months ago?" I asked. He placed the knuckles of his fist against the bridge of his aquiline nose as if hesitant to respond.

"After the fact, yes. And I'm sorry. A cousin of mine went rogue. Said he was getting back at some of your guys for—well, to be honest, I don't even know what the reason was that time. For as long as I can remember, there's always been something going on."

"I guess I'm not being straightforward enough," I said. "I just need to know, were you ever involved in any of the sabotage against us?"

"Never." he said, looking me straight in the eye. "Though, to be honest, it was nothing noble on my part—I just think there are more important things to do in life than pick fights with the neighbors." He walked back over to me and brought his face level with mine.

"Like what?" I asked. The intensity of his gaze caused my voice to catch in my throat.

"Like teaching you an important life skill," he said, teasingly. I followed him, almost hypnotized, as he led me over to the counter next to the stove. Standing behind me, he guided my right hand to the bowl of whisked eggs. "No one is born a great cook. You learn by doing it," he whispered into my ear.

"Is that your pick-up line with all the girls?" I asked nervously, not certain I actually wanted him to answer. Our arms moved in tandem as he guided me to empty the contents of the bowl into the cast-iron skillet. I felt giddy and breathless.

"No, actually," he replied. "Come to think of it, I've never cooked for a girl before. This might sound funny, but it's kind of a personal thing for me. So I guess that'd make you . . . my first." His breath felt like a gentle breeze on the back of my neck. I was glad he was still standing behind me and couldn't see how flustered I was by his nearness, his touch.

Though we were silent for the next few minutes, the air around us buzzed with electricity. Roman helped me tilt the frying pan, and we watched the egg mixture flow evenly over the mushrooms and begin to set at the edges. Then, gently grabbing onto my waist, he directed me to one side so he could put the pan in the oven. "So, I'm just going to say this," he finally blurted out, glancing tentatively at me as if he was about to bare his soul. "I don't want you to leave. I know it might sound crazy, since we only just met, but here's the thing: I've never felt this way about anyone." His face looked more resolute now, as if he was relieved to have just shown me all his cards.

"I don't want to have to leave, either," I whispered, feeling a frisson of anticipation as he pulled me closer. "Especially not now. Now that I've . . . found you."

I'm not certain how long we stood there in the kitchen kissing after that, but the dinging of the oven's timer eventually brought us back to reality. Using a dishtowel to grasp the handle, Roman removed the pan from the oven and set it on the range before returning his focus to me. "You're staying, and so is Cap's," he said, his voice sounding determined. "We just have to figure out how. And we *will*."

Minutes later, he escorted me to a two-top in the dining room.

"Your lunch, m'lady," he said, placing the frittata in front of me with an exaggerated flourish.

"Mmm," I said, after taking a bite. "It's delicious. Maybe I'm a decent cook after all."

"Or maybe you just finally found your 'passion,'" he said, raising his eyebrows suggestively. I smiled, and lifted my glass to him in flirting assent. His culinary remedy had worked, allaying both my rumbling stomach and my frazzled nerves. Now, instead of dwelling on my earlier anguishing news, I focused on getting to know Roman as we chatted at length about our crazy Italian families, school, and work. We even got into a good-natured debate about whether the Caputos or Montes could truly claim bragging rights on the best pizza.

"I'm telling you—my *bisnonno*, he pretty much invented the deep-dish pie."

"Your *bisno*-what?" I said.

"My great-grandfather. That's what we call him. Are you *sure* you're really Italian?"

"Hey! Them's fightin' words," I teased, picking up a sprig of arugula and tossing it at his face. He dodged the airborne roughage. "I'll have you know my blood runs marinara red!"

"Truce! Truce!" he said, laughing. "Let's not add any more fuel to our families' fire."

After helping him wash up the dishes, I held my glass of Pellegrino and scanned some of the family pictures hanging up in the small cupboard-sized office located off the kitchen. On a cork bulletin board, I identified a photo of Roman wearing a cap and gown—his eighth grade graduation, no doubt. The tall, lanky blond boy standing beside him was clearly the guy in the faux tux T-shirt that Ty had almost pummeled last night.

"How'd you get a blondie in the family?" I asked, tapping the picture.

"Oh, that's Mark," he said. "Not related, but he's a waiter here. We go to school together, too. He's the funniest guy I've ever met. He loves to hear himself talk, and mocks me endlessly, but there's no one I trust more with my secrets. He already knows about you, actually." I faintly detected the color brightening on Roman's cheeks, and I was certain that I had just blushed even deeper.

"Well, in any case, you looked cute in braces. What a baby face!"

"Shut up."

"I'm serious!"

I glanced again at the wood-paneled walls, which featured a laminated poster detailing how to perform CPR and the Heimlich maneuver, a computer-printed schedule of the staff's upcoming shifts, framed but faded newspaper write-ups, and a whiteboard on which someone had scrawled, "Mario Puzo is my homeboy." A Chia Pet showing no sign of its promised plant life sat atop the dented gray file cabinet in the corner. On the shelf above it, old bowling trophies cohabitated with two stacks of blank food order pads and a bottle of homeopathic sleeping pills. More yellowed snapshots were taped onto the side of the file cabinet, and I didn't pay them much mind until one, in particular, caught my attention.

"Who is that?" I asked. "This pretty girl with the blonde hair?" The face smiling back looked somehow familiar to me.

"I don't know. It's been up there for as long as I can remember. I assume she's some distant relative, but I couldn't say who," he said, before pointing at a clock on the desk next to the filing cabinet. "Hey, it's one-forty. Didn't you say you needed to be somewhere at two?"

My heart withered a little. I didn't want my first date with Roman to end just yet. Then again, maybe it didn't have to. The sleuthing I planned to embark on this afternoon *did* involve him, after all. Asking him to accompany me was a little risky, but then again, good judgment is never the hallmark of one newly in love.

"What time are you due back here for work?" I asked.

"Four-thirty."

"Here's the thing: I'm curious to find out what sparked our families' legendary feud," I said. "It probably won't amount to anything, but at this point, there's no harm in trying. Wanna come along?" He took a wide stance in front of me so that our faces were on the same level plane. Grabbing both of my hands, he looked deep into my eyes as if he was trying to say so much more to me than the two words that were about to escape his lips.

"I do."

CHAPTER 12

I Am No Pilot

THE NEXT MORNING, Benny and I stood among the jumbled throngs of other young men in a poor attempt at a line that extended almost four blocks in length. Our intended destination: the Army Air Corps recruitment office. Enlisting for our country was a given, as natural a reflex as blinking in the wind. And while I was champing at the bit to have a go at Hitler, Mussolini, and Tojo, I simultaneously harbored some intense qualms about the route we were taking to do so.

"I don't know, Benny. When I get my marching orders, I prefer to be, well, *marching*. I was thinking infantry, or maybe a nice armored tank division."

My pal brought his arm down heavily on my shoulder.

"Where's the glamour in that? Give me the 'wild blue yonder' any day."

"Easy for you," I said, craning my neck to note our progress in line. For my friend, there was no question about which branch of the military needed our able bodies. Growing up, Benny had kept a veritable squadron of model airplanes on shelves in his bedroom, not to mention scrapbooks full of flying machine pictures he'd clipped from various periodicals. He could still spend hours sticking his nose through the fence at the Municipal Airport watching planes land and take off. As for me, the only thought worse than spending the duration of the war 25,000 feet off the ground was the thought of spending the duration of the war without Benny, which is why I stood anxiously in line with him. I knew there was no guarantee we'd get to go through this thing side by side, but one thing was certain: I'd stick with him for as long as I could, come hell or high altitude.

"In my pilot's uniform, I'm going to need my *own* armored tank division just to fend off all the babes who will be throwing themselves at me," Benny boasted, before glancing at me hesitantly. He knew immediately what I was thinking. "And, seriously, Nick, just think of your wedding day—how spruce you'll look in your dress uniform—probably decorated to hell with medals when this is all over."

Proposing to Stella had been out of the question following yesterday's earth-rattling news, and it now remained off the table indefinitely. In the blink of an eye, the future of millions of Americans had been branded with a giant question mark. Naturally, no one wanted to think the worst, let alone voice it aloud. I hoped that Stella would wait for me, and I was certain that I would return home—no Axis power could keep me from her after all I'd already endured. Still, given the nature of war, baiting Stella with the potentially illusory promise of a life together just didn't seem fair. That discussion would have to wait. So, too, would the business. Pizza was no longer our priority.

We finally made our way inside the packed recruitment office, and Benny and I each checked in separately with harried officials who sat behind makeshift folding tables. I removed my homburg hat out of respect—unnecessarily, as it turned out. The uniformed gent sitting across from me didn't so much as look up from his paperwork as he quickly rattled off a series of questions that didn't stray too far from name, address, and date of birth. (Since he didn't inquire and seemed disinclined to care, I opted to not point out my paralyzing fear of heights.) After ceremoniously stamping an official-looking form—*ka-chunk!*—the Army clerk unceremoniously pointed to the far end of the room, where makeshift medical exam rooms were cordoned off by gray-green hospital curtains. An eye chart recitation, blood pressure check, and stethoscope sounding later, I was back out on the sidewalk waiting for Benny, having been instructed to await my assignment, which would arrive via mail in four to six weeks. Considering I was still slightly shell-shocked from my hasty enlistment, I wondered how I was ever going to cope with the *real* chaos surely awaiting me in battle. I figured Benny would emerge mere seconds after me, but a good fifteen minutes later, I was still waiting. No doubt the loudmouth was already trying to buddy up to those recruiters in the hopes of skipping ahead from aviation cadet to sergeant. That'd be just like him.

"Thank God," I said when he finally appeared. "Let's go get lunch—I'm starving."

"I'm 4F," he said, his face ashen.

"Like hell you are," I said, pushing him in the back, which sent him stumbling forward a few paces. If Benny was physically unfit for service, then I was a monkey's uncle. "Let's hit up that deli my ma's always raving about."

"They didn't take me, Nick. They said . . . they said something's wrong with my ticker."

"Wrong how?"

"It doesn't beat in the right rhythm," he said with a sad shrug.

"What, so you'll never be a jazz drummer? Malarkey. You're *fine*," I said. "Better than fine! You always have been!"

"That's what I told them! Who cares how it beats, if it beats for the red, white, and blue, dammit!" He placed his hands and forehead against the side of the brick building. I walked over to him so that I could lower my voice.

"Okay, so maybe they don't want you flying a plane. Then you'll do something else. They've got to need plenty of tactical support on the ground, right?"

"They won't take me," he said.

"Then you try the Navy. It doesn't matter which—"

"Stop, Nick. The docs in there—they said I could drop dead in an hour or, more likely, seventy years from now, but that no branch of the service was going to take that risk."

I swallowed hard and stared at the ground, crestfallen on Benny's behalf, and only just beginning to comprehend how ironic our situation had become. I, the guy who couldn't stand on my toes without feeling lightheaded, was heading into the Army Air Corps to fulfill all of Benny's childhood fantasies, while he'd just been permanently grounded.

* * *

"But all that perfect Italian hair," my mother lamented on the afternoon of my departure for boot camp. "Why would they want to shear it off like they're farming you for wool?"

"Don't worry, Ma," I said, smiling as I sighed. "I'm pretty sure it'll grow back."

"Well, you'll still look handsome in your uniform, of that I'm sure," my mother crowed. "Isn't that right, Stella?"

"I'll say," my girl answered quietly. She hadn't spoken much today, and I understood why. We had been saying our tearful goodbyes for the last five weeks, and the anticipation of my imminent departure was near excruciating for us both. It's why we had mutually decided that Benny would be the one to see me off at Union Station. Stella didn't want to risk going to pieces on me in public when I boarded the bus; instead, she'd agreed to stay behind with my ma, whose combination of pride and grief rendered her an emotional shambles. Cooking food was one of the few ways she knew how to express her feelings, which is why she'd packed me an embarrassing smorgasbord to take on the bus ride to Missouri, despite our just having eaten the home-cooked lunch to end all lunches.

"I hope my seatmate doesn't mind the smell of garlic and oregano," I said, leaning down to give my mother a peck on the cheek as she handed me my care package. Benny's whole family had come over from across the hall to wish me well.

"We'll miss you, Dominick," said Mrs. Caputo, giving me a hug.

"Give 'em hell, kid," mumbled Benny's dad, his teeth gripping a cigar. Benny had been downright mortified to tell him that the United States military had rejected him, as if his so-called "ailment" branded him an ineffectual weakling. Unfortunately, I knew my departure would be yet another opportunity for Mr. Caputo to belittle my best friend.

"I guess we'd better be shoving off, eh, Ben?" I said, bending down to grab my small, beat-up suitcase. I caught Stella's eye, and she blinked hard, then shifted her gaze to the floor. She reached her small arm around my mother's ample shoulders, which had begun to shake as her tears started. I knew Ma was remembering my father's death and wondering if the same thing was going to . . . well, never mind.

"I'll only be one state away, Ma," I said. "It's just basic training. You could probably shout out the window and I'll hear you."

"Just be safe, *tesoro*," she sobbed into the rose-embroidered handkerchief Stella handed her. I caught my girlfriend's glance one more time and made the gesture of scribbling with a pen in the air. *Write me?* She nodded her head fervently and smiled, tears now escaping from her eyes, too.

The bus's engine idled at the terminal as the driver loaded luggage into a compartment underneath.

"Be ready to work when you get back," Benny instructed me. "I'll probably have pizza parlors open all over the city by then."

"Sounds good to me," I said. "Now remember, you've got to leave the faucet on a trickle when the weather's below freezing, otherwise those pipes will burst."

"I'll worry about my taps, you worry about yours," Benny said, forcing a chuckle. "Antonio's is going to be just fine. I'll put my kid brothers to work, and Vera's offered to help out, too."

"Don't let Carmen get too close to the stoves. I'm always telling her she's going to burn herself."

"Nick, I've got this."

"And look after Stella, too," I said, more seriously now. "Especially, well . . . especially if—"

"If nothing," Benny said, dismissing me with a wave of his hand. "Don't be such a belaboring basket case."

"Oh yeah? Well an ill-bred, indolent invalid like yourself shouldn't talk."

"At least I won't look like a beetle-headed measle in that garrison cap you'll soon be sporting."

"You're right. You'll be more along the lines of a puny, three-legged miniature schnauzer."

"So says the chicken-skinned, humped-back hobgoblin." Benny's voice started to crack as he said this. He feigned a cough and looked away. This was even harder than I thought it was going to be. I reached into the pocket of my overcoat and handed him a small brown paper bag that was folded over on itself.

"Hold onto this for me, will ya? Until I get back?" Benny took a glimpse inside at the bag's contents.

"Whoa, Nick—are you sure?" He looked genuinely surprised.

"Positive."

"Okay. But it'll be here when you get back, safe and sound. Trust me on that." Our eyes said those things that seemed fitting in a time such as this, even if we both knew it would be too hokey to put it into words. The bus driver shut the luggage compartment and gave me a nod as he walked toward the front of the bus. It was time. I extended my hand, businesslike, to Benny as people around us exchanged waves and hurried embraces with one another. The bone-chilling Chicago wind had picked up, and as it sliced across my face, my eyes started to water. A stint in the balmy South Pacific might not be *so* bad, I thought to myself. Where fate landed me from here was anyone's guess.

CHAPTER 13

I'll Pay That Doctrine, or Else Die in Debt

"JUST TO BE CLEAR—you're sure she's not going to bludgeon me with a leg of prosciutto?"

"Uh . . . I don't *think* so?" I conjectured, considering Roman's question. "She tends to stay above the fray. You'll see. And, besides, I'm pretty sure she would *never* want to waste perfectly good prosciutto."

"Well, there's that, at least." I knocked loudly on the front door of Carmen's apartment near the Medical District. An eternity seemed to elapse as we waited for a response.

"She's a little hard of hearing," I explained to Roman, rapping again on the door.

"That's okay, I'm in no rush," he said, enveloping me in his arms, his chest against my back. He leaned his head over my shoulder and kissed my cheek.

I laughed, and was about to kiss him again when I heard the deadbolt click. Roman and I moved apart and hastily composed ourselves as the door swung open.

"Gigi! What brings you over here?" Carmen asked. "Won't I see you in a few hours?"

At her age, it was a sheer marvel the way she continued to bust her butt for my family at the restaurant when she ought to have rightly retired from Cap's decades ago. But considering we

133

were the closest thing she had to family—she had never married and didn't have any relatives living nearby—Carmen took great pride and joy in coming to work every night and socializing with familiar faces, including the longtime customers who specifically requested her section of the restaurant. She was as much a part of the fabric of Cap's as the pictures on the wall or the secret spices in my great-grandpa's recipes. It pained me to imagine what would become of her if the restaurant left Taylor Street. Waiting tables made her feel like she still had something to contribute to Cap's, and despite my mom's best efforts to assign her less laborious tasks, Carmen always insisted she wasn't ready to be "put out to pasture." Nevertheless, Dad typically sent her home early most nights (with takeout containers of leftovers from the kitchen). While the spring in her step was a bit less, well, springy these days, it still impressed me the way she could remember not just so many of the usuals that our repeat customers ordered, but also personal details of their lives, from birthdays to grandkids' names. That memory was exactly what I was hoping to mine with this surprise afternoon visit. Crossing the threshold of her apartment, I gave my coworker a quick hug, which brought me face to face with the Sacred Heart of Jesus picture hanging on the wall behind her. Whether it was the eyes that seemed to follow you wherever you went or the heart engulfed in flames, something about that image always unsettled me.

"I just thought I'd swing by, because there are a couple things I'd love to ask you about and, well, work might not be the right time or place for it," I said. "This is my friend Roman, by the way."

"Last night was so wonderful," the wizened waitress gushed. "Father Vito can dance his pert little tushy off!" I raised my eyebrows and turned to Roman, whose face registered a similar mild astonishment. Carmen made the sign of the cross as if to absolve herself, then swatted her hand as if to change the topic. "Well, come in Gigi *and guest*," she said. "Would you like a treat?"

She produced a decorative glass bowl with colored hard candy in cellophane wrappers that probably hadn't been touched for a decade.

"No, thanks, we just ate," I said.

"Roman," Carmen said thoughtfully, as if trying to put two and two together. "Roman, Roman, Roman . . . aren't you a . . . ?"

"Monte?" I finished her question.

"Yes, ma'am," Roman hastened to respond. "I'm the youngest son of Joe and Peggy Monte. Before you say anything, I just want to let you know that—"

"Are you sure I can't get you a scoop of ice cream—maybe a Coke float?" Carmen interrupted. Ever with a sweet tooth, she was far more incredulous at our refusal than at seeing me with our sworn enemies' son.

"No, thanks, Carmen. I brought Roman with me because, well, we were hoping you might be able to tell us a little something about the feud between our families. You've been working at Cap's since Grandpa owned the place, right?"

"Mm-hmm."

"And . . . ?" I asked, expectantly. Carmen smiled artlessly, clearly not picking up on my cues to dive right in with the answers we were looking for. "What I mean is, do you remember anything—anything at all—as to why Grandpa Sal started hating them?"

"Oh, it didn't start with him," Carmen replied. "He disliked that family from womb to tomb, God rest his soul."

"You mean it's been going on since *before* Grandpa? Any idea why?" I prodded.

"The mind is a funny thing," she said. "Sometimes I can't remember what I had for dinner two nights ago, but I can tell you exactly what I had for breakfast the morning we found out the war was over. It's a matter of looking in the right file." She knocked upon her forehead with her knuckles. "All seventy-six years are in here somewhere." She winked and smiled at Roman with such evident enthusiasm that had she been sixty years younger, I might have called her out for flirting with my guy. After inviting us to sit down, she launched into a few interesting anecdotes about her childhood but revealed nothing specific about what caused the mutual hatred to flare up between our two families.

"The bottom line is, I was only a child when the trouble first began," she finally responded. "Whatever caused such bad blood between the Caputos and the Montes wouldn't likely have been appropriate for small ears. As I got older, well, no one dared mention the Monte name in passing. It's not wise to open old wounds, as they say." Her words hit a nerve. Were Roman and I snooping for the key to a box that was best kept closed?

"I know your families might not agree with me, but as far as I'm concerned it's all water under the bridge," she continued, smiling. "You seem like a nice enough young man, after all. And you're certainly easy on the eyes! So the two of you are an item, I take it?"

"Uhhh . . . ." I stammered. Had there been a rock in her apartment I would have crawled under it.

"Not that it's any business of mine," she continued, with a twinkle in her eyes, "but I was beginning to wonder if Gigi would ever—"

"Okay, Carmen, *thank you*," I preempted her, mortified.

"Since you asked," said Roman, "we kind of are . . . an *item*. Or we'd like to be. But, as you can probably imagine, we're not quite sure how we can get everyone else in our families on board."

"Just be patient—only fools rush in," Carmen responded. "You know I feel a very deep loyalty to your parents, Gigi, but when it comes to this feud, I have to admit I feel a lot more like Switzerland. I only wish I could be of more help, but I'm rooting for you, kids. I really am. Don't let anyone else dictate your fate."

"Easier said than done," I sighed. It had been so long since Carmen had been my age that she must have forgotten, in some ways, how complicated it was to still be beholden to one's parents.

"See you down at Cap's soon," I said, scooting off her oversized floral sofa to say goodbye.

"Let me at least wrap up some peanut brittle for you two to take home with you," she said, turning toward the kitchen.

"Please, Carmen, don't trouble yourself," I said, following her. She was already rooting through a cabinet in the kitchen when a photograph in her dining room seized my attention. In a stand-up frame on the shelf of a glass-fronted hutch, behind a menagerie of Hummel figurines and porcelain teacups, was the same five-by-eight picture of the beautiful young woman I'd seen in the photo at Monte's.

As I stared in bemused fascination at the image, Roman came into the room and stood beside me.

"Carmen," I called out, "who is this blonde woman in the photograph out here?"

"What kind of question is that, silly girl?" she shouted back while clattering through a drawer full of Tupperware containers. "Why, it's your great-grandmother, of course!"

I turned to Roman and saw that he looked as wide-eyed as I felt. My dad's grandmother had died before I was even born, and while I'd seen pictures of her (including some that hung on the walls of Cap's), I hadn't made the connection. In older age, she had white-gray hair, wore glasses, and was thicker around the middle. Certainly not the glamorous-looking woman in the picture! Carmen was now standing in the doorway leading to the kitchen. "That's the one memento I asked to keep when she died," Carmen continued, "because it's exactly how I remember her looking when I was a little girl. Such a beauty . . . and a real spitfire, too—unlike that wet-blanket older sister of hers."

Carmen appeared to be a bit misty-eyed as she gazed at the picture. "You know, your great-grandmother was the one who always warned me against getting married," she said. "I never quite understood why, but she said it would only amount to heartache.

I never met my Mr. Right in the end, so I guess I took her advice. But . . . I'm not sure she had it right." There was a hint of regret in the old woman's face, as if her mind (or perhaps her heart) was somewhere far away.

When Roman and I got back out to the sidewalk in front of Carmen's apartment building, compulsory peanut brittle in hand, we couldn't contain our excitement.

"Why would *my* family have a picture of *your* great-grandma?" he asked.

"This just took a very weird turn," I agreed. "You don't think we could somehow be related, do you?" We looked at each other in horror, but then Roman flashed a sardonic grin.

"I'm sorry, it's just too ludicrous—like the plot of a really bad TV movie," he said. "I mean, I *know* who my great-grandparents are, Gigi."

"Okay, you're right," I said, breathing a sigh of relief. "But it's still very, very strange. There's obviously a connection there. Do you think your grandfather would know more?"

"My great-granddad, more likely."

"Oh yes, your *bisnonno*."

"Ah! We have a fast learner."

"Yeah, well, we don't speak much of the mother tongue in my family. I mean, you saw what *my* great-grandma looks like: as Presbyterian as they come."

"And a hottie, too," Roman remarked.

"Hey!" I teasingly punched his bicep.

"What? She is! Or, was, I should say."

"So what do we do now?" I wondered. "Can you ask your great-grandfather?"

"Absolutely, but even if he remembers—and that's a big if—he might be in no mood to dredge up the past where your family is concerned," he said. "He lives at that nursing home over by the university. I'll pay him a visit and see if he can shed light on any of this."

"Great. I have no idea where this will lead, but . . . ." Suddenly the enormity of the situation hung over me once again. How long could I really keep my parents from knowing about Roman?

"We have to do *something*." He finished my sentence before taking my hand. "I know. I feel the same way."

"I should head back to Cap's. They'll be wondering where I am," I said, after checking the time on my phone.

"I'll walk you to the train station." He pulled me closer to him. "On the way, we can talk. You promised to tell me the story behind your name."

* * *

Back at Cap's, I went about my daily prep work for the first time in a month, all while striving to avoid Chef's impatient, searching glances. He was obviously dying to debrief me about my day, but attempting to fill him in as my parents scurried in and out of the kitchen and hovered near the pass-through would have been asking for trouble—as if I possibly needed any more. Besides, my dad's stony demeanor reminded me that I had far more pressing problems than trying to broker peace with my would-be boyfriend's family. An ax was hanging over Cap's, and if it fell, the Caputo/Monte feud would be a moot point. With fate literally forcing my hand, I sent a short, but decisive, text. I still had hopes that if I followed every possible avenue, I might find one that led to a solution we could all live with.

I popped a piece of sourdough bread in my mouth, an old culinary trick to prevent tears, and proceeded to chop red onions. About midway through the task, my cell vibrated with a response. It was Perry—he was in the alley waiting for me. I chose a moment when Chef and Mario were mid-bicker to wipe my hands on a towel and sneak off.

Wearing baggy purple basketball shorts that revealed pasty, skinny calves, Perry stood at the top of the stairs out back, his arms folded across his chest. Less than twenty-four hours ago I was standing in this spot swooning over the boy of my dreams. Now I was attempting damage control with my worst nightmare.

"So, what do you want?" he mumbled. I silently ordained him with my new favorite Perry moniker, The Incredible Sulk. He was clearly still ticked about last night. I hadn't really thought out how I was going to approach this conversation, but the "more flies with honey" tactic seemed like a good place to start.

"Thanks for coming," I said. "I wanted to apologize about last night."

He didn't say anything, but I thought (or hoped!) he looked slightly less annoyed.

"So," I ventured, walking up the steps toward him. "I heard things went a little south between your dad and mine this morning."

"You shouldn't be surprised," he said, staring past me at the brick wall.

"But I am. Your dad seemed to be having such a great time at the party last night. I can't help but wonder what changed. If there's been some sort of misunderstanding, then maybe we could—"

"I wouldn't call it a misunderstanding. 'Misled' might be the better term."

"Oh. I see." It didn't take a master at inference to read between these lines. He was ticked off that I'd given him the cold shoulder. Roman's rescue mission hadn't helped, either, of course. But that couldn't have been what led his father to yank all our funding. Could it?

"You said you had an apology?" Perry asked with a note of impatience in his voice. I blanched. I'd only waved that olive branch to try and get things back on the right foot—at least between Rich and my dad—but I wasn't about to apologize for anything that I'd said or done to him the evening prior. And I most definitely was not going to apologize for Roman.

"Things got a little crazy by the end of the night, granted," I said. "I should have been a better hostess. You brought me a rose, after all!" I plastered a chipper smile on my face as I said this. He remained stone-faced, like some wax figure at Madame Tussauds.

"Did your dad put you up to this?"

"No, honestly!"

"Well, then, riddle me this: Who was that dude who came up to us in the hallway?" he asked. "The one who said he was your boyfriend?"

"Who? Oh, him," I waved my hand dismissively and scoffed, camouflaging my inner disgust at the fact that he thought I owed him an explanation. "I didn't even know his name!"

"Really?"

"Uh-uh. I mean, I was just as surprised by that whole thing as you were!"

"Oh." One corner of his pouting mouth gave a barely perceptible uptick, as if he was weighing this new information. Though I hadn't exactly lied to Perry, I wasn't sure how far I wanted to take this conversation. On the one hand, if I could fix this whole falling out with Perry's father, maybe we wouldn't have to ship out to Peoria. On the other hand, letting Perry believe he still had any sort of chance with me, romantically speaking, just made me feel sick to my stomach.

"What are you doing tonight?" Perry wondered, his tone of voice markedly less harsh. At least this time I actually had a valid excuse.

"I'm needed here, alas." I motioned down at my work attire.

"Your dad told me last night that he'd give you the night off if you ever wanted to, you know, hang with me."

"No offense, Perry, but I think my dad's opinion on that front may have changed sometime between last night and this morning." (Duh. I couldn't believe I even needed to explain that fact.) "And with the money trouble Cap's is in these days," I added, "I really need to pitch in."

"Money problems? You mean the loan my dad wants repaid, ASAP?" Perry smirked as if he was semi-amused by the whole situation. "Pops can be a real Shylock, I'll grant you. But that's not to say it can't be sorted out."

"Really?" I asked, attempting to ignore his blatant use of a racial slur. "Do you mean that?" I dubiously wondered what might be required of me to remedy my dad's financial troubles.

"Let's just say I can be pretty persuasive where my dad is concerned," he slowly responded, "if I had the right motivation."

"If?"

"Well, I mean, now that I stand corrected about the situation with your pseudo-boyfriend last night, I think we can make this little situation just—poof!—go away." He made a sleight of hand gesture with his revolting, spindly fingers.

"We?"

"We. As in you . . . and me." He inched closer, staring too suggestively at me with those creeper eyes of his.

"Can't we just be friends?" I asked, though I suspected I already knew what his answer would be.

"Friends?" He rolled his eyes at my suggestion. "If you want to save your dad's restaurant, you're going to have to give me more than that. A *lot* more." Though my recent involvement with Roman was as complicated as quantum physics, Perry's suggestion—and my response to it—couldn't have been more black and white. My choice was clear.

"You're disgusting," I said, turning to go back down the stairs. As I opened the back door to Cap's I offered one parting word of advice. "Next time you're in the market to buy a girlfriend, try the Dollar Store. They come a lot cheaper, there."

One thing I knew for certain: I would rather spend an eternity in purgatory (or Peoria) before I'd endure another minute with Perry.

CHAPTER 14

Sad Hours Seem Long

"WHERE THE HELL ARE YOU GOING, PANCAKE?" Smitty whispered to me, shivering underneath his threadbare rags. "The latrine, again?"

"Nah—I just need some fresh air," I said, tossing him my poor excuse for a blanket so he could double up and keep warm.

"If they come across you out there, you'll be cruisin' for a bruisin'."

"Yeah, so. What else is new?" I grumbled, clambering over two more guys sawing logs between me and the open doorway. I would have grabbed my boots and put them on, but my captors had confiscated them months ago when I had arrived in this godforsaken cesspool. The open blisters covering my feet could attest that barefoot life wasn't as idyllic as Mark Twain had made out in my favorite childhood classic, *Huck Finn*, the plot of which I had replayed over and over in my mind during these many days of my captivity. Exiting our ramshackle barracks, which made a chicken coop seem like the Taj Mahal, I crept over to a palm tree near the barbed wire fence and collapsed against it. I knew they'd be rousing us before dawn with the business end of their Arisaka rifles and screaming at us in Japanese— not exactly the reveille you look forward to each morning. I ought to have been at least trying to get some shut-eye so I could somehow endure tomorrow. But a rain-free night like this one provided me with a rare temporary respite from all the pain and terror.

My stomach churned. Hunger pangs or, perhaps, a harbinger that I'd soon be back hunched over the squalid hole in the ground we'd affectionately nicknamed "The Gents' Room." When the agonizing abdominal pain I'd grown accustomed to didn't materialize, I chalked it up to the mere side effects of starvation. Funny thing about nicknames. I'd earned my new moniker after the ritual stunt I enacted each morning at "breakfast" (a meager portion of maggot-infested white rice).

"Mmm-mmm," I would loudly enthuse, digging into our revolting repast and grinning at my fellow prisoners. "Tastes *just* like pancakes!" It was the sort of thing Benny would have said. I'd come to rely on the memory of his goofy antics and optimism during my time here. *What crazy thing would Benny do in this scenario? What outrageous nicknames would he come up with for the bastards who tortured us daily?* Thoughts of my pal back home helped keep my spirits from landing somewhere down that Gents' Room hole—but just barely.

Glancing up at the sky, I marveled at the beauty of the countless stars twinkling overhead. They naturally made me think of one person in particular: Stella. It would be mid-afternoon back in Chicago, and I tried to imagine what she might be doing: taking in a movie with a girlfriend, shopping in some posh boutique on Michigan Avenue, or maybe just curled up by the fire reading one of those sci-fi dime-store novels she went on and on about.

"*Lizard Goddess of Lake Neptune?*" I'd once teased her, holding the paperback just out of her arm's reach.

"Give it back, you! This'll be considered classic literature one day, I'll have you know." She circled around my back, then under my arm as I dangled it just overhead, until I finally caught her up in my embrace. She was laughing and rosy-cheeked, but when she stopped laughing and looked at me with those baby blues that had turned suddenly serious, my pulse raced. "I don't care if I get the book back," she chided, "but if you don't kiss me right now, it will go on your permanent record." The memory seemed so far away now.

There went my stomach again. It sounded like an angry tomcat howling. When I got back home, the first thing I'd eat was one of our pizzas loaded up with plenty of ham, pepperoni, and our homemade *salsicce*. One pie wouldn't be enough, though, so I'd probably eat two, then finish it off with a big fat piece of apple pie with a slice of cheddar on top. As always, my thoughts drifted back to Stella. Benny and I had laughed at her that day when she thought pizza would resemble a dessert pie. But why couldn't it? All these days stuck out here in the jungle as a "guest of the emperor" left me hungry for the biggest, densest pizza pie imaginable. When I got home, I'd stuff a pie tin to the brim with pizza ingredients, load it up with sauce, cheese, and even more sauce on top, for good measure. A *deep-dish* pizza—yeah . . . that would hit the spot. If I made it back—when I made it back—I'd be more like Benny and swing for the bleachers every time.

Before the war, I'd had a lot of fears, but they all seemed laughable in retrospect. I was no longer afraid of any of the things that used to scare me. Now they only made me laugh. Flying, for example; I'd give anything to still be up above the clouds in my own little dream world. Nothing up there was so bad as what was down here. I knew that, now. During primary flight training back in Arcadia, Florida, the first plane I flew in was a single engine prop with a two-seat open cockpit—a bona fide Red Baron kind of deal that would have driven Benny mad with jealousy. I cursed him as the instructor sped us down the runway—*What in God's name did you rope me into?*—but once I felt the sensation of the ground dropping away and the tops of the trees came into view, an adrenaline rush kicked in. Leaving the world behind, I decided right then and there to jettison all my fears and doubts along with it. On a wing and (admittedly) a few prayers, I was reborn.

It was eventually determined that I wasn't quite pilot material (go figure), but given my head for numbers and general punctiliousness, I became an onboard navigator instead. I was trained in determining a plane's position using only onboard instruments, a technique known as "dead reckoning." But by far, the most fascinating skill I learned was being able to plot our location using a sextant and the location of stars in the sky.

"Men have been able to navigate by the stars for three thousand years," our instructor had explained. "Your controls may fail you, but the stars never will."

Stella. We'd been exchanging letters faithfully every month right up until the bombing mission that went awry. The bundle of letters that I normally kept with me in a pocket of my flight suit had disintegrated into mush while I drifted in the Pacific, but it didn't matter. I'd memorized most of them.

My darling Nick: The sun and I are on poor terms these days. Watching it set over the city skyline makes me jealous, knowing it's run off to greet you without me. I wish I could stop the earth from spinning at just the right point on its axis so that my twilight and your dawn could mingle. Better yet, I wish I could spin the earth back in time, to that night overlooking the river when I first said, "I love you." Since I can't whisper it into your ear again, I whisper it to the heavens and hope you can somehow divine my thoughts from so far away. Oh, Nicky, when I finally see you again, I won't let you out of my sight for even a second. Until then, I must make do with cutting remembrances of you into little stars that shine on me always, guiding me through each day until your return. I live as if in a dream, only to truly waken when you come back to me. Yours ALWAYS, Stella

Desperate to get a message to Stella after arriving in this abhorrent limbo, I'd managed to come by a scrap of paper and a nub of pencil, with which I wrote to her. The boys chided me, saying only a fool would think our tormentors might actually post some sad sack's love letter home. Nevertheless, I needed to let Stella know (to let anyone know, really) that I was here, that I'd survived the plane crash. I'd humbly presented my letter to one of the younger soldiers who kept guard over us. He had an unreadable face, but unlike most of the others, he didn't appear to take sadistic pleasure in our suffering. I'd been holding onto a glimmer of hope that he'd actually be willing to help me, but when I covertly handed him my letter, he merely glanced at it, crumpled it in his hand, and tossed it in the dirt. And with that, my glimmer of hope had disappeared completely.

The air was frigid, but I tried to enjoy it. Nine hours from now, it would feel like I was standing inside old Bessie—maybe even hotter. If I got out of this mess, I knew I would never be the person I once was. Though I was becoming physically weaker and weaker, I swore to myself that I was only getting tougher mentally. I was being forged into steel, and the Nick that emerged from this wouldn't be the diffident, self-doubting Nick from years past. Maybe that was the whole point. I was being turned into the man who would make Stella proud, my mom proud, my father . . . .

Perhaps it was just the delusional effects of exhaustion and malnutrition, but sometimes the faint rustle of tree leaves or the way the long, wild grasses bent in the wind told me my dad was here with me. He was right behind me, just as he had been when I was first learning how to ride a bike, when I thought I'd never get the hang of it. "*Don't give up,*" his voiced seemed to whisper. "*Just keep going. You can do this. Don't give up.*"

CHAPTER 15

Beautiful Tyrant!
Fiend Angelical!

"WHAT DID YOU SAY?" Chef paused midway through deboning a chicken to aim a withering glare at Mario.

"I was just suggesting you should—"

"Not. Another. Word."

"But—"

"Shush, *you*!" Chef practically shouted at the maître d'. "If I want your opinion, I'll ask for it. This is my domain, remember?" He waved his cleaver to indicate the area around him. "Yours is out there, *capiche*?"

Mario backed out of the kitchen with his arms raised in surrender and a "no one ever listens to me" look on his face.

Our first night back in business since the *Zwaggert* critic's disastrous visit wasn't off to a smooth start (and I was still shaking with anger after my encounter with Perry), but Chef and Mario's bickering was at least a return to normalcy. On the bright side, there was some good news to offset reopening night jitters: Our reservation book was respectably inked-in for the dinner rush.

Mario said he expected a decent number of walk-ins, too, and reminded us more than once to turn tables as quickly as we could without giving guests the obvious bum's rush. The bad news (besides everyone being on edge): Ty was late for work, which meant I had to cover my section *and* pinch-hit with Carmen and Aunt Val to cover the tables that were normally my cousin's jurisdiction. Carmen moved pretty slow, and Aunt Val was preoccupied by Ty's whereabouts. That left me to pick up most of the slack, and only a few stolen moments in which to think about my illicit new boyfriend.

Lucky for me, Chef was by now bursting at the seams to get a detailed summary of my afternoon with Roman. Like a gossip-hungry love junkie, he peppered me with questions any time I passed through the kitchen.

"So you saw him today?" he asked while draining a huge pot of boiling fettuccine. "Did you talk to Carmen, like I said?"

"Yeah, and yeah." I grabbed a chrome-plated pizza tray stand in my left hand and used my other to affix a pan gripper onto the side of a hot-from-the-oven deep-dish order.

"And . . . ?"

"And Table Twelve is going to chew my arm off if I don't get this pie out to them. I'll tell you about it later. Where is Ty, anyway? Did anyone check the office phone to see if he left a message?"

"I expected him here early," replied Chef. "He said he wanted to come learn how to make my recipe for pasta fazool."

My mom, who had just approached the pass-through window to clip up another order, glared at me. (She'd been in a horrible mood all day.)

"Gigi, Angelo, enough chitchat. Get back to work," she said. Chef and I exchanged glances of shared resignation and went about our business.

By nine-thirty, the dinner slam had subsided to a trickle, which was typical for a Sunday night. A handful of tables were still occupied by parties enjoying their entrées or dessert, but it was a relief to know the day was winding down. Finally starting to feel the effects of my sleep deprivation and cute-boy infatuation, I volunteered to help Mario wipe down all of our thick laminated menus. It would at least get me off my feet.

"Would you call it a success?" I asked him as we sat in an empty booth near the entrance.

"We had more customers than I imagined we'd have," Mario said. "The month off doesn't appear to have hurt our returning business, but I'm not the authority on the matter." He nodded in the direction of my father, who stood behind the bar. Dad was lovingly polishing the wine glasses, inspecting them for any unseemly smudges. He looked not so much happy as wistful in his work as he returned the glasses to hang by their stems from the overhead rack.

I set aside the menu I was wiping and walked over to the long wooden bar where I plunked myself down on one of the red leather stools.

"What'll ya have?" my dad drawled, propping himself onto his elbows and smiling at me.

"Grappa?"

"Yeah, right," he scoffed, picking a cocktail cherry from a condiment tray and popping it in his mouth. "I'd like to see you try swilling that stuff. Need I remind you that you're sixteen, not twenty-one?"

"I can't believe Ty's MIA our first night back," I said, changing the subject.

"I'd say I could kill him, only your Aunt Val will probably do it for me," he said. "That boy is always begging me to let him have more responsibility around here, and now this? He's just too much of a wildcard, that one." As he groused about Ty, I metaphorically kicked myself for bringing up the subject. Even though my cousin wasn't speaking to me at the moment, he was still the closest thing I had to a brother, and I wasn't about to throw him under the bus.

"Dad?" I said, changing the subject.

"Yeah, sweetie?"

"Is everything going to be okay? With Cap's, I mean?" My earlier conversation with Perry continued to unnerve me. Had I done the right thing in summarily rejecting his offer?

"Times are tough, but there were tough times for your Grandpa Sal and his dad before that," he answered. "If we stick together, we'll come through it all okay. Cap's may be a restaurant, but it's a family first."

"But if we had to close for good . . . ."

"Never," Dad said, looking more serious now. "This restaurant is your legacy, and I'm going to do everything in my power to make sure this is all yours one day, even if we have to . . . well, it's not something you need to worry about."

I wondered if it would take some of the pressure off my dad if I finally confessed to him that I didn't *want* the responsibility of running Cap's someday, that it wasn't *my* dream and never had been. Though it would relieve my own inner burden, such a shocking admission would probably only make matters worse, I reflected. The sound of street traffic outside caught my attention, and I swiveled on my stool to see two uniformed police officers walking through the double doors. It wasn't unusual for the men in blue to swing by for a carb-laden dinner when they got off duty.

"Dave! Charlie!" said my dad as they approached, anticipating their first order by reaching for two glass beer mugs.

"Evening, Ben," one answered in response, clearly not in the mindset for drinks. "I'm afraid we've got a situation."

* * *

My parents refused to let me join them when they accompanied Aunt Val, Frankie, and Enzo to the hospital to see my cousin. Dad claimed it was too late, and Mom insisted they needed me to help close up the restaurant. But the real reason, I knew, was that they were trying to protect me from what I might have to face if I went with them. Ty was in critical condition, the cops had explained to my father. In a state of shock, I'd instinctively jumped off the barstool to go find my Aunt Val, but not fast enough to avoid hearing the words "head trauma" and "brain swelling" tangled up in their devastating dispatch.

Twenty minutes later, I was bawling my eyes out in the back of the restaurant, resting my head on Chef's shoulder the way I used to as a little girl when things had seemed unbearable. In hindsight, my problems back then had been sweetly insignificant: the sting of a skinned knee, the wounded pride of being told I was "in the way," or the anger of having my favorite doll flung onto the telephone wires in front of the restaurant by my cousins. Chef would sigh his soothing, "There, there," lift me up onto the counter and pull a cherry Popsicle from the freezer, thus restoring order to my fledgling little universe. I longed for the days when my problems were so trivial. Last night I'd been caught up in a spiral of existential angst about falling for the wrong boy, and now, almost impossibly, something worse had happened. The fleeting thought of Roman tugged at my soul—an urge to find him and tell him what happened, to have him assure me, in that way of his, that everything would be okay.

"'Head trauma.' I mean, that's *really* bad on the scale of bad things," I said in full freak-out mode as I helped Carmen and Chef clean up the kitchen for our early closing. "No one's called us yet. That's got to be a good sign, though, right? If there's nothing to really worry about, then they wouldn't feel the need to call. Or it could be the opposite, and they just can't face telling us that—"

"Jumping to conclusions is a good way to stumble and fall," Chef advised me, sternly. He'd been very quiet since we'd gotten the bad news. "Let's just wait until we hear something definitive. Your father will call as soon as he is able to."

"Angelo's right. Don't you worry, Gigi," said Carmen, her gentle, careworn eyes trying to bolster my spirit. "I've lit so many votives to Mother Cabrini in my lifetime, the old broad owes me a big favor at this point."

I wasn't sure if saints worked that way, like a broken vending machine bound to offer up a boon of saving grace if you just fed in more quarters and banged hard enough. But whether Carmen was right or not, I figured there was no better time than now to start praying.

"Let him be okay," I silently beseeched God who, so far at least, seemed to be pretty fickle in who he helped out in this world. He couldn't manage to keep people from starving or countries from killing each other, so was he really competent enough to save my cousin? I sent a second mental shout-out to my Uncle Greg, Ty's father, just for good measure. Maybe he had the wherewithal, wherever he was, to fix this by putting in some cosmic request. I half-shuddered at the fact that tonight didn't feel too different from that morning four years ago when we'd found out Uncle Greg had suffered a heart attack in his sleep. Neither saint nor deity had bothered themselves to intervene that night, and Ty and his two younger brothers had been twisting in the wind ever since. No one really wanted to admit that my cousins' antics had transformed in recent years from typical boyhood precociousness to something darker and somehow more troubling. But we'd all seen it. I know death is a part of life, but my three cousins had gotten a raw deal losing their dad. Whatever his faults, Ty shouldn't have been fighting for his life in some hospital bed. He'd already suffered enough.

Carmen and I froze in our task of disinfecting the counter when we finally heard a cell phone ring. It was Chef's, and he retrieved it from the pocket of his gray checkered uniform pants. I strained to hear the voice on the other end of the line while simultaneously struggling to interpret Chef's less than telling responses.

"Holy Mother of God," he slowly said, making it impossible to decipher whether the news he'd just received was good or bad.

"Is he okay?" I said loudly, frantically beckoning so that Chef might at least shoot me a simple thumbs up. (He didn't.)

"Uh-huh. I see," Chef continued, holding up the palm of his hand to silence me. "At least he's not in any more pain." I felt a chill run from my tailbone up through the base of my neck. "'Not in any more pain'" as in heavily medicated, or "'not in any more pain'" as in *dead*? I wanted to tackle Chef to the ground in order to rip the stupid phone out of his hand and talk to my father myself. Instead, I waited as Chef began asking questions. "Medically induced? So how long will they keep him like that? And they're sure they can bring him out of it when his condition improves?" *Thank God. At least he was still alive.*

Mario, who'd been putting the front of the house back in order, poked his head through the swinging kitchen door at that moment.

"Gigi? There's a young man out front who says he needs to see you."

Roman. My eyes began to brim with tears, prompted both by sadness and some strange semblance of relief. We hadn't planned to meet up tonight. Crazy as this sounded, I knew he must have sensed how much I needed him. Still, I was surprised that he'd come back to Cap's, knowing he was *persona non grata* after last night, and, if we're being honest, long *before* last night, too. Something didn't seem right.

The dining room was deserted when I entered, save for the skinny blond guy standing by the bar. He was facing away from me, but I knew in an instant who it was.

"Mark?" I asked, approaching him. He turned to face me, startled by the sound of my voice. His upper lip was bruised and swollen, and there was a large abrasion across his forehead. "Where's Roman? Why are you here?"

"You know who I am?"

"Yes, you're Roman's friend. Where is he?"

"He sent me here to tell you," said Mark, his voice starting to tremble, "it was an accident." Accident? No. He couldn't mean . . . .

"Where is he?" My throat started to constrict. I didn't want to acknowledge the obvious implications, the dots that were beginning to connect in my mind.

"They took him away. I told him—" With his thumb and index fingers, Mark rubbed the outer corners of his eyes as if to stop the tears in their tracks. His expression was a strange combination of anger and grief. "—I told him not to get between us. But your cousin had me pinned. I couldn't . . . ."

"Ty?" I felt my skin ignite like a hot furnace, and my arms started to shake. "You? And Roman?" I could hear the tinge of hysteria in my voice. "*You* did this to Ty?"

"No! I mean . . . Roman was confused and out of it when the cops showed up, and now they think he's responsible, but they're wrong. He did it . . . but he didn't. It just happened. Ty fell, but Roman didn't push him. I swear."

"*Push* him?! What are you talking about?"

"That's what I'm trying to explain. We were at Polk station," Mark answered. He looked confused, as if he thought I'd already know all these details. Suddenly it all came together: The 'L's' Pink Line station on Polk Street was elevated, perched like a bridge about thirty feet over the road. Only a waist-high metal railing separated the train platform from the street below. I didn't want to hear any more. I wanted Mark to be gone.

"Get out," I said, stepping forward, my arms outstretched as if to shove him. It was only the eviscerating mental image of Roman, doing the same to my cousin, that stopped me from laying my hands on him. "Get out!"

"Roman was trying to keep *me* from going over," Mark tried to explain. "Your cousin was totally out of control. Roman had my back, and—"

"Get out!" I yelled louder.

"It's not his fault!" Mark shouted back, trying to make his point clear. "He just wants to you to know that—"

"*Get out!*" I screamed it this time, at the top of my lungs, with a forcefulness that stunned even me. The kitchen door flew open and Chef and Mario came running to my rescue. Mark turned, fleet-footed, and escaped through the front door. This couldn't be happening, I told myself. This couldn't be real. Through my tears, I assured my friends that no harm had come to me. At least, no harm in the physical sense. The emotional damage, however, was catastrophic.

"Just tell me about Ty," I said, hoping for some good news. "What did Dad say?"

I used to be afraid to go to sleep. I was petrified that I'd stay in my dreams and never wake up. Whether it was a nightmare—or even some perfectly pleasant alternate reality—the idea of being stuck in a limbo land, powerless to return, struck me as the most horrible thing that could happen to a person. Other girls marveled dreamily over Snow White and Sleeping Beauty, but those fairy tales freaked me out to a level that some might consider paranoia. A shrink would probably have a field day with it, but I still slept with my bedroom door cracked open, if only to give me the comforting sense that I was never fully committing to "the other side." When Chef explained that doctors had placed Ty in a chemically induced coma—on purpose—to protect his brain from the swelling caused by the injuries to his skull, I felt as though my veins had been injected with ice water. It was like that paralyzing sensation your nerves suffer when you jump into a too-cold swimming pool for the first time.

"The treatment is a good thing," Mario said, trying to reassure me. "The doctors are doing everything in their power to make sure Ty comes through this okay." But his words brought me no comfort. The anguish I felt over my cousin's accident was like being lost at sea. Just when I'd think the pain was too much to endure, the thought that Roman was responsible came crashing over me like another giant, suffocating tidal wave. I was drowning in an immeasureable grief.

CHAPTER 16

No Warmth, No Breath,
Shall Testify Thou Livest

ONE OF THE BEDTIME STORIES MY DAD LIKED TO
tell me before he died was about Rip Van Winkle, an ordinary
guy who fell asleep in the woods one day and slept for twenty
years. When he woke, everything in his universe was frighteningly
strange and unrecognizable. Man alive, could I relate. I hadn't
been asleep, but had spent the last two years living a nightmare. It
was autumn of 1945, but it certainly felt like two decades later on
this, my first day back where I belonged. Only, I didn't feel like I
belonged—not at all, in fact. For starters, no one had been waiting at Union Station to pick me up. Not that I'd expected the city
of Chicago to throw me a ticker tape parade, but it felt markedly
anticlimactic to take the bus home. The military had sent Ma a
telegram weeks ago letting her know I was returning to Chicago,
but when I'd tried phoning her from Honolulu, and again in San
Francisco before I'd taken the train back east, she failed to answer
in both instances. It was probably for the best that my arrival was
unanticipated. Had she known the specifics, my mother would
have planned a colossal banquet for three hundred and fifty of our
nearest and dearest. Considering everything I'd been through, I
wasn't quite ready for that kind of Italian celebratory onslaught.

Exiting the bus, my heart leapt at the sight of the old place
on Taylor Street, which looked relatively unchanged. I entered

the front foyer and climbed the creaky wooden steps, but my homecoming knocks went unanswered. After rapping on the door across the landing, I heard the sound of footsteps approaching from within. I smiled in anticipation of seeing Benny or his parents, but instead, the door opened to reveal a middle-aged woman I didn't recognize. Glancing over her shoulder, I noticed an overstuffed davenport in the living room that looked equally unfamiliar, and drab brown curtains now hanging from the front bay window that would have made Mrs. Caputo frown in condemnation.

"Hello. Uh . . . are any of the Caputos in?"

"Wrong apartment," the woman said, beginning to close the door in annoyance. Benny and his parents had moved? What rabbit hole had I fallen down?

"Wait," I said, putting my hand in the doorframe to prevent her from shutting the door in my face. "I live across the hall here, or rather, my mother does." I pointed across the landing. She stared at me blankly.

"Mr. Twardowski lives there," she corrected me, shaking her head. "Are you sure you've got the right street, mister?"

I descended the steps and reemerged back out on the sidewalk, feeling stunned and confused. There were times during my long internment that I thought I was losing my mind, and here I was again, completely doubting my sanity. I felt like Odysseus— doomed to endure ordeal after ordeal when all I wanted to do was just get home. And, apparently, home was now located . . . somewhere else.

Heaving my rucksack over my shoulder, I headed east toward South Racine Avenue, attempting to formulate a plan. I briefly entertained the notion of schlepping across town to Antonio's, but it was Sunday—the place was sure to be closed. Thanks to lingering side effects of what the Army docs diagnosed as beriberi, my joints ached and my knees still buckled from time to time. I didn't have much more walking in me today. Noting a pay phone across the street, I stepped off the curb to cross over when a familiar holler made me halt in my tracks. Swiveling on my feet, I spied old Mrs. Deluca leaning out from her first story window. She'd been a fixture in that open sash since I was a kid, and as such, was one of the neighborhood's most trusted sources of gossip. Wearing the same blue housecoat and hairnet she always did (I guess some things *hadn't* changed since I'd been away) she gaped at me and gesticulated wildly, like a melodramatic opera diva playing to the nosebleed section of a crowded theater.

"*Non ci posso credere!* It's like looking at a ghost! Wait there!" She disappeared from her window ledge after indicating that she was coming outside to welcome me. I knew I looked gaunt and sickly—months of dysentery and starvation will do that to you. But likening me to a ghost seemed brutally blunt, even for an old Sicilian matron. At least she might be able to tell me where in tarnation everyone was.

"Dominick Monte!" she cried, grabbing the stone balustrade as she inched her fragile body down the front stairs. I bounded up to steady her, grabbing her by the elbow. "Oh! Oh! God save us all, is it really you?" (Did I mention she had a flair for dramatics?) Clearly she had heard about my epic saga, but I was in no mood to recount all the horrific details—especially not to the Taylor Street tattler.

"I'm fine, Mrs. Deluca, but where is everyone? It's like they all up and vanished. My ma, Benny Caputo . . . I just really want to find them. And see my girl." A curious look passed across Mrs. Deluca's face, as if that whole ghost remark hadn't merely been a figure of speech.

"You don't know?"

"I've been in a P.O.W. camp for the last nineteen months, ma'am. I'm afraid I don't know much these days." She pursed her lips, tactfully, and that's when I knew something was terribly wrong. The last year and a half—all those nights I'd spent wondering if

I'd even survive another day—surely no news on the home front could rattle me like that had. I'd hung on for thirty-two hours treading shark-infested waters after our B-17, christened "Fair Rosaline," got shot down over the Pacific. I'd endured torture and daily humiliation at the hands of my captors after one of their "rescue" ships finally scooped my near-lifeless body out of the cold, choppy waters. I even watched my fellow prisoners—American and British soldiers—die slow and agonizing deaths right before my eyes. Yet now, the ominous silence of Taylor Street's most notorious busybody left me with the chilling sensation that my nightmare wasn't quite over.

"Your mother has been staying with friends out in Cicero," Mrs. Deluca explained. I knew exactly whom she was referring to, as my mother's best friend from high school, Alma Rizzo, lived in that suburb just west of the city.

"And what about the Caputos?" I asked. I couldn't wait to tell Benny about my new idea for the pizza place—the concept Stella had inspired, a singularly American pizza pie, in the most literal sense of the word. I just wanted to revel in normalcy again. After what I'd been through I didn't want, or need, much more than that.

"Benito?" As she pondered this, Mrs. Deluca prodded her hair at the nape of her neck, tucking it further up into her hairnet, as if hedging. "He opened up a new place over on the corner of Taylor and Ashland," she said. "They live in the apartment above it." So that was it. Benny really had done it. As good as his word, he'd opened another location of the pizza joint while I was away, the old rascal. "But Dominick," she continued, "maybe you shouldn't—"

"Nice seeing ya again, ma'am!" I said to Mrs. Deluca (and she truly had no idea how much I meant that). She looked at me with real concern in her eyes as I turned on my heels to seek out my pal. Never mind that, I thought to myself. A few weeks of Italian home cooking and I'd pack on enough pounds to erase any worried looks aimed in my direction. I tamped down the feeling that some awful knowledge was awaiting me just around the corner. After all, given everything I'd been through, it was no wonder I was a tad circumspect about reacclimating to civilian life.

When I got to Ashland Avenue, I was looking for the facsimile of our neon sign, the one we'd hung at the original Antonio's location. Instead, I was greeted with a marquee almost three times its size emblazoned with a flourish of cursive letters: Cap's Restaurant. Cap's as in Caputo? Okay, Mr. Fancy-Pants. Way to commandeer the limelight. A copy of the menu was posted behind a glass placard on the wall near brick stairs that led down to the restaurant's front entrance. I gave it a passing glance, only to notice that this didn't seem to be a casual pizza joint so much as a fine dining establishment. There were entrées I recognized as being among Mrs. Caputo's specialties. Well this was a change for us . . . but, surely, this was progress! Entrusting Benny with the business had clearly paid off. Peering inside the darkened basement restaurant and seeing how la-di-da the whole place looked, it occurred to me that he and I were one step closer to "big time." He hadn't simply held down the fort while I was away—he'd built a palace while he was at it!

Remembering that Mrs. Deluca had said the family lived on the second floor, I pushed open an entry door to the right of the restaurant and climbed a flight of stairs that led me onto an elegant landing. I rang the buzzer, observing the expensive-looking wallpaper and brass door knocker as I waited. Benny had done all right for himself and his folks! When the door opened, the face of an angel appeared—a startling but welcome surprise.

"Stella?! Sweetheart!" I exclaimed. "What . . . what are you doing here?"

I dropped my rucksack to the floor in anticipation of our embrace, but with a shrill scream, she collapsed onto the ground—

echoing the thud of my bag. Before I could stoop to help her up, a voice called from another room.

"Darling! Are you okay?" He emerged at the end of the hall and his feet skidded on the hardwood floor when he saw me. His face, at first registering alarm, turned to absolute shock.

"Benny?" I looked at my friend, utterly confused. Stella, her arms thrown around my ankles in supplication, was sobbing and shrieking uncontrollably. Benny wilted onto an upholstered armchair next to a phone alcove in the wall, burying his head in his hands. Then I saw it. In the alcove, next to a ceramic pot filled with African violets, was a sterling silver picture frame. And in it, a wedding photo of a gorgeous, if tragically familiar, bride and groom.

My harrowing ordeal in the camp had been hell on earth, but when we were finally liberated, and I realized I was going to live, I felt invincible. My enemies had tried, but failed, to stomp out my soul. No worse fate could befall me, or so I had thought. Despite the pain and degradation I had suffered, I had held onto hope—to the image of her sweet, smiling face. Thoughts of Stella and our future together had been my lifeline. And now, as with the single stroke of an ax, that rope had been severed. Staring blankly into the fuzz-covered leaves of those rich purple violets, I felt an odd sensation deep in my chest, as if my inner pilot light had just been snuffed out. What little remained felt cold and desolate.

CHAPTER 17

A Madness Most Discreet

"I CAN'T UNDERSTAND WHY THE POLICE AREN'T PRESSING CHARGES. Roman Monte ought to be in jail for attempted homicide," Ty groaned. I sat by his hospital bed four days after the accident, gripping his hand. Doctors had brought him out of his coma less than forty-eight hours earlier, but even in his weakened condition, he still had vengeance on the brain. A brain, which, mind you, had sustained one doozy of a beating. The way his head was now wrapped up in medical gauze, his younger brothers had taken to calling him "Q-Tip," but only after his chief physician double and triple assured us all that there were no signs of permanent damage to his brain tissue. In addition to a hairline fracture of his skull, Ty had broken three ribs, punctured a lung, and shattered his elbow, which would require reconstructive surgery at some future date, but he would recover, thank God.

"Apparently, two people who were on the platform Sunday afternoon thought Roman looked like he was trying to keep you from going over the railing, not push you," my mother explained to Ty. It was the first I'd heard of these developments, and my heart skipped a beat.

"But that's incredible!" I inadvertently exclaimed. My relatives who were gathered around the bedside stared at me, expectantly, but I decided it would be wiser to remain silent.

"It's an utter travesty. Why anyone would believe unreliable eyewitness testimony over the actual victim's statement to the police is beyond me," Aunt Val finally said.

I darted my eyes back and forth, as if I was counting marbles on the floor, then cleared my throat.

"I'm going to go get a soda," I said, trying to maintain my mental equilibrium. "Anybody else want one?" The disappointment on Ty's face as I excused myself made it clear he knew full well what my unexpected outburst was really all about.

The snack stand in the hospital's main lobby had a long lunchtime line, but if I was being honest, that's not why I'd come down here anyway. I pulled my phone out of my purse and called Roman for the first time since the incident. He hadn't attempted to reach out to me, having clearly received the message I sent via Mark that I wanted him permanently off my radar.

"Gigi?" He'd picked up on the first ring, sounding almost dazed.

"Hey, Roman."

"Your cousin—please say he's okay."

"It's hard to tell by looking at him—you'd think he'd fallen from ten stories, not two. But the doctors seem to think he's out of the woods. I'm at the hospital now."

"You must hate me." His words made my heart wince. It was true; I had hated him, reviled him, cursed him with a teeth-gnashing intensity. But I'd also been bombarded with emotions that were the exact opposite of hate: concern, empathy, and a complete inability to exile him from my mind. The resulting guilt I felt over those conflicting emotions had almost consumed me this last week.

"I don't hate you, Roman."

"But . . . I thought . . . ."

"Because I know you didn't push him. No matter what Ty says." He didn't speak. All I could hear were short and choppy intakes of breath. I recognized what I was hearing, because I'd reacted the same way when I'd finally learned that Ty was going to live. The muffled sounds coming from the other end of the line were sobs of relief.

By the time I hung up with Roman a few minutes later, I saw Chef walking down the hall from the main entrance, carrying a couple of Cap's catering bags full of the lunch he'd promised to bring over.

"How's the patient?" he asked.

"Grumpy, which is a good sign," I answered. "I'm sure he'll cheer up when he sees real food."

"Garlic rolls and gnocchi with vodka sauce—his favorite," said Chef, nodding his head toward his cargo. "Hey, make yourself useful. Take one of these bags, will ya?"

"Actually . . . I'm not going back up to the room. I have to take off." Chef gave me a look as if to say, *You're up to something; do I even want to know?* I shook my head to confirm that he was indeed probably better off being left in the dark. "Will you just tell them I had to go check on something?"

"Some*one*, you mean," he admonished.

"It's not like that," I pleaded. "I just . . . I *need* to go do this."

"You're playing with fire, Bird."

"I know," I sighed, not even attempting to counter him on that point. "All I'm asking is that you don't add more grease to it. Can you cover for me? Just this once? It will be the last favor I ask of you, after all." Chef's sad eyes at this remark let me know he had relented. Disappointing me—especially now—was beyond the scope of his abilities.

"Don't make me regret this," he said. "Get to Cap's when your shift starts—or else. Your family needs you right now. Remember that."

I rapped on the glass door of Monte's, despite the black-and-white *Closed* sign that hung directly in front of my face. A shadowy figure inside opened the door, allowing me to slip into the dark and deserted eatery. While an intense chemical attraction had been the hallmark of our earlier interactions, this moment felt somehow deeper; more profound. Having been pushed to the brink of my emotional limit, I desperately needed a soft place to fall, and I found it in Roman's arms. From the way he held onto me, as if clinging to a lifeline, I suspected he felt exactly the same way. Only the sound of birds chattering in the trees outside penetrated the silence of the moment until I finally spoke.

"I can't stay long. My family would freak out if they knew I was here."

"I'm glad you came. I really needed to see you." He looked beaten down and exhausted.

"Roman, look—Ty's brothers, Frankie and Enzo—well, I've never seen them so riled up. You need to be careful, at least for these next few weeks, until . . . ." The news was still a freshly opened wound to me. I wasn't sure if or how I'd be able to tell him.

"I understand that they're angry, Gigi, but you have to know: Ty came after *me*," said Roman. "He must have seen us together at the station." I remembered my cousin's threat the night of my party and what he said he'd do to Roman if I ever saw him again. "I tried to talk to him, but he wouldn't listen. He just started throwing punches. Then Mark showed up and pulled your cousin off me. I thought Ty was going to kill him. I had to do *something*."

Roman looked at me imploringly. "We struggled by the railing, and when I sensed him going over, I tried to hold onto him. Honestly, I did. It all happened so fast. He hit the blacktop below, and . . . Christ," he whispered, "I thought he was dead." It was clear he'd been mentally replaying the terrifying moment many times during the past four days.

"He got lucky," I said. "Ty's tough, thank God. He's had to be."

"I'm sorry, Gigi." His weary eyes closed as he slowly shook his head. "I'm so incredibly—"

I placed my fingers to his mouth to stop him from speaking. His lips—so soft and warm . . . God, this wasn't fair. When he kissed my palm, everything I'd planned to say to him slipped from my mind. Shrugging my purse from my shoulder, I let it drop to the floor. Keys, lip balm, and loose change toppled out onto our feet, and we gave in to the kiss as though we were both under some powerful spell. All the angst, sadness, and confusion that I'd been feeling in recent weeks vanished, like entering an airlock that shielded us both from the past and the future. If I could only stay here like this, with him, none of this other madness could reach us.

Entwined in his arms, I pressed my body even closer, giving myself over completely to the sudden impulse I felt to melt into him.

Threading his fingers through my hair, he gently caressed the back of my head as his lips pressed urgently against mine. His other hand slowly moved along the waistband of my jeans until it rested flat on the curve of my lower back, just under my blouse. The warmth of his touch against my skin sent a ripple of pleasure up and down my spine, but as I felt his hand slide back around and up toward my ribcage, reality started to flood back into my brain like a jarring submarine diving alarm. I was getting in too deep.

"Roman," I finally said, pushing myself away from him and placing my forehead against his chest. My heart was beating so hard I thought it might bust open my ribcage. I inhaled deeply to catch my breath. "I can't."

"Is it because of what happened with Ty?"

"No." I looked at him imploringly. "Yes. I mean, that's part of it, but it's so much more than that." I slowly, wistfully, backed away from him and stooped to the floor to collect my purse.

"If I could explain to your family how things actually happened—" He lowered himself next to me, grabbing both of my hands in his. "—maybe they'd understand. Maybe you and I could . . . ." He didn't complete his thought, no doubt realizing the foolishness of what he was suggesting.

"Nothing can fix this, Roman," I said quietly, rising to my feet and taking one step backward. I pointedly averted my gaze. "Our families are never going to accept the idea of you and me. We can only . . . be thankful it will be over soon."

"Over soon?" He repeated, straightening back up.

"That's what I came here to explain," I said, my voice beginning to waver under the weight of what I was about to say. "My dad made the decision yesterday. We're taking over the lease on his cousin's building and closing the Taylor Street location. I'm moving."

The pain I saw in his face mirrored the inner angst I'd been feeling ever since Dad made the announcement in the kitchen before last night's dinner service. With our restaurant in the red and the anticipation of who knew how many thousands of dollars in Ty's medical bills, my father had come to the conclusion that we couldn't just go on treading water without taking some concrete step to stem the proverbial blood loss. My life was unraveling like threads in a poorly knit sweater.

"When?" Roman asked, sliding his hand over his jaw.

"As soon as possible, if my dad gets his way. The plan is to move by the beginning of August, so I can start the new school in September."

"But that's only a few weeks away!"

"It could be even sooner. As soon as Ty gets out of the hospital, basically."

"When do you think that will be?"

"It's hard to say. He's pretty messed up." I thought about my cousin lying broken in his hospital bed. The truth was, Ty's physical injuries almost seemed to be an outer manifestation of the inner pain he'd been struggling with since his dad died. He'd been looking for trouble for years. Had it not been Roman, I suspected Ty would have just as easily found another outlet for his inner demons. I also suspected that Roman's sensitivity and tact prevented him from telling me about previous provocations he and his family may have suffered at the hands of my hot-tempered cousin.

"I can't believe you're leaving," Roman said, walking to me and enveloping me in his arms. I burrowed against him, realizing it would probably be for the last time. "It feels like the world just keeps caving in on itself."

"I barely even know you . . . so why do I already miss you so badly?" I looked up into his eyes as tears began to brim in my own. I fought the urge to let them fall, not wanting our final moments together to be marred by the memory of me losing it. "Do you think we'll ever see each other again?"

"Of course we will," he said, pushing a strand of my hair behind my ear. Though he sounded completely confident, I'm not certain either of us believed it. "It's not *that* far," he continued. "Besides, nobody stays with their family all their life in this day and age."

"Nobody *except* for Italians."

"Then we'll be the gypsies who do it differently. We'll secretly run off together when the time comes, like Bonnie and Clyde, minus the bank robbing and machine gun toting. I'm betting some day we'll be able to laugh about how dramatic it was when we first fell in love."

"'In love.'" I let the phrase reverberate off my tongue. "So that's what this is."

"It's the only logical explanation for how upside-down my whole life feels right now," he said. Having a boy tell me he loved me should have been one of the happiest moments in my life, but instead, all it did was intensify the hurt. The realization had dawned upon me that, for a whole slew of tragic reasons, we were doomed.

"I do love you, Roman." I squeezed my eyes shut as I said this, because it was suddenly too excruciating even to look at him. "But the thought of leaving Chicago is unbearable, and if I leave a piece of my heart here, too, I honestly don't know how I will even survive all this."

"What are you saying, Gigi?" He released me from his grasp and stepped away, slumping down onto a long wooden bench near the front window.

"I'm saying that this needs to be goodbye." I lowered myself next to him. "We can't drag this out. It would only be torture for us both."

"So this is it? I just met you, and now I'm never going to see you again?" Roman stared straight ahead. I knew it was pain and not anger that made his expression appear as though it had been carved from stone.

"Maybe we'll be together someday," I said, reaching out to hold his hand one last time. "But right now, we just can't," I whispered. "I can't." And with that, like a candle that had just been snuffed out, I had reluctantly banished the only boy I ever loved.

* * *

A few hours later, while doing routine prep work at the start of my shift, Frankie and Enzo brought their two-man goon squad to my end of the counter—as if I needed any more grief today.

"What you did this afternoon, Gigi? Not cool," said Enzo.

"I don't know what you're talking about," I responded, quartering and chopping heads of romaine.

"Your not-so-stealth mission to see the guy who practically murdered our brother," Frankie chimed in. "Yes, we know." I glanced down the counter at Chef, who shook his head ever so subtly to indicate that he hadn't betrayed me. "It's pretty obvious from the way you've been acting all week that you're taking your boyfriend's side in all this."

"He's not my boyfriend, and my heart is sick over it, by the way; just as my heart is sick over what happened to Ty. I'm sick of it all!" I set down my knife and turned to face them. Though the twins were trying to puff out their chests the way their big brother usually did, their scrawny butts didn't intimidate me in the least.

"I'm half inclined to tell Uncle Benji what's going on between you and him," Enzo declared.

"Oh yeah?" I stared him down, almost laughing aloud at his pointless threat. "And what's he going to do, ship me out of town to some distant relatives? In Peoria, maybe?" No more thrilled to be moving than I was, Frankie and Enzo exchanged withered looks. They'd begged their mom to let them stay behind in Chicago to finish out their high school careers among their friends. My Aunt Val's answer had been an unequivocal no. Though she had married into the Caputo family, twenty-five years had made her one of us. My mom and dad had helped support her, both emotionally and financially, following my Uncle Greg's death, and she felt she owed it to my parents to stand with them during the family's unanticipated crisis. United we stand, divided we fall, and all that.

"This might not mean much to you," I said, addressing my cousins in a more conciliatory tone, "but I don't know what I would do if the two of you and Ty weren't coming along with us to the new place. It's the only thing that even makes any of this—" I couldn't finish my thought, as yet another torrent of tears hit me. Where my crying jags were concerned, it had been monsoon season this week.

"Aww, Gig—it's going to be okay," said Frankie, wiping his hands on his apron and pulling me in for a hug.

"I'm sorry, you guys," I said, glancing at Enzo, who bit his lower lip in concern at my mini breakdown.

"Don't cry, Gigi," he said. "You're right. God knows none of this will matter anymore, two months from now. I'm sorry I even went there with you and the whole Monte thing."

"I hate that we're moving to *stupid* Peoria," I sniffled into Frankie's shoulder, still thinking of the boy I was leaving behind.

"Oh, but we're going to kill it there," said Enzo.

"Yeah," said his brother. "We'll be like rock stars in that podunk town, Gigi. The locals will genuflect in awe at our mind-blowing good looks, and they will hang on our every word as if we are prophets—"

"Demigods—" Enzo clarified.

"Thank you, Francis, yes, *demigods* from some far-off civilization. Don't get snot on my shirt, by the way, cousin. Nose crud on one's clothing does not play in Peoria, as they say." I obediently lifted my face off his shoulder.

"You'll have a whole new, unsuspecting market for your stupid boy band karaoke routine," I conceded.

"There you go! Why didn't we think of moving there ages ago?" said Enzo. "To hell with Chicago. Peoria is my kind of town! Ol' Blue Eyes got it all wrong, man!" With that, the twins launched into an improvised version of the famous Sinatra anthem for the city of Chicago, changing the lyrics, clunkily, to Peoria, as they sang into kitchen tongs they'd pilfered from hooks above the stove. I wiped the remnants of tears from my cheeks and tried, but failed, to laugh at their sad clown antics. Maybe someday I'd figure out how to feel happy again.

CHAPTER 18

Why the Devil Came
You Between Us?

STELLA TRIED TO COMPOSE HERSELF, rising shakily and smoothing her skirt—as if decorum even mattered at this point. Benny stood up from the chair he had originally collapsed onto, seemingly in disbelief.

"Nick—you're alive."

"And you're . . . " I paused, glancing between his face and hers. " . . . married." She clasped her still-trembling hands behind her neck and gazed up, wearily, as if seeking some divine intervention from the decorative plaster medallion in the center of the ceiling. Benny's footsteps made the only sound as he walked into the living room and opened a wooden secretary. He returned, unfolding a small piece of paper. I could see "Western Union" emblazoned across the top in large black letters.

"They sent this to your mother, but she couldn't bear to keep it," Benny said, handing it to me. "I asked her if . . . if I could hang onto it."

THE SECRETARY OF WAR DESIRES ME TO EXPRESS HIS DEEP REGRET THAT YOUR SON SECOND LIEUTENANT DOMINICK MONTE HAS BEEN REPORTED MISSING PRESUMED KILLED ON EIGHT OCTOBER OVER

SOUTHWEST PACIFIC AREA STOP IF FURTHER DETAILS OR OTHER INFORMATION ARE RECEIVED YOU WILL BE PROMPTLY NOTIFIED STOP

J. A. ULIO THE ADJUTANT GENERAL

The telegram was dated the twelfth of October, 1943—Columbus Day. It made me sick to my stomach to think of Ma receiving this devastatingly blunt missive sometime during the course of the annual Taylor Street festivities. So this was their excuse; I'd been taken for dead. I can't say such a scenario had never occurred to me during my long internment, but I hadn't given the possibility much real credence. Japanese officials had taken down my name when I'd first arrived in the camp, and I had imagined, at the time, that the U.S. Army or the Red Cross would somehow be notified of my whereabouts.

"I prayed it wasn't true, Nicky," Stella said, her voice cracking, "I bargained with God. I begged, and I pleaded, but everyone told me, over and over, 'He's not coming back, Stella. He's *never coming home.*' Finally, I had to accept it. The Army eventually sent some of your personal effects. I had no idea—"

"What in God's name happened to you?" Benny interrupted her. "How are you . . . here?"

"Our plane got shot down off the coast of Guam. A Japanese torpedo boat dredged me up and hauled me off to an internment camp. That's where I've been."

"For *two years?*"

"Damn it, why is everyone acting so thunderstruck that I'm alive? I know for a fact that Ma got a telegram after we were liberated."

"Telegram? That's impossible," Benny insisted. "Your mother didn't get any telegram. She would have let us know something like that. She would have notified all of Cook County with news like that."

"I'm certain it was sent," I muttered. "I was standing right there in the ship's radio room when they sent it! I've been trying to call her, too, but apparently she's not living at the old place on Taylor Street anymore."

"She said all of the memories there were just too upsetting," Stella explained, filling me in on what I'd already discovered a half hour earlier. "She needed to move on."

"Just like you, apparently," I muttered.

"Nicky, please." Stella averted her eyes, once more. She couldn't even bring herself to look at me.

"How long did you wait after this?" I said, shaking the telegram at her in anger. I could feel heat rising up my neck and into my face. "A month? Maybe two? Or was this news exactly what the two of you needed to feel better about what had probably started up long before this telegram ever arrived?"

"Don't, Nick. Just don't." Benny positioned himself between Stella and me, and placed both hands on my shoulders, not so much threateningly as beseechingly. But I wasn't finished with Stella.

"I don't care what this telegram says!" I shouted, craning my neck to see around Benny so that I could stare her down. "'Missing' isn't dead."

"You were 'presumed killed!'" she cried.

"Presumed? Presumed isn't a certainty," I argued. "All this time, I was desperately clinging to hope—the hope of a future with you—just to get through each wretched day. Why? Why couldn't you have done the same thing for me?" The colors in the room melted into a hazy mixture, and I began to feel woozy, drunk on my own tears. How could I be back on U.S. soil and yet still feel so tortured? "Were you in love with him this whole time? Because you said it was *me*. You said *I* was the one you loved."

"And I did, Nicky. I do! I mean . . . oh God, why is this happening?"

"Sweetheart, you're getting too upset," Benny said, reaching for her hand. The familiarity of their touch twisted my stomach into knots. "Nick, we can discuss this man to man, but now isn't the time. I think you ought to just leave."

"Oh, here we go again. Benny's got the girl, now Nick has to scram. It's the 'sacred pact' all over again. You know, I see what this is all about. First, she wasn't good enough for you, so you dumped her. Then the second you found out she actually meant something to me, you just couldn't stand to see me happy, could you? You had to steal her back, just to prove a point. Or maybe just to prove what you've always believed: that you're better than me."

"Cut it out. It wasn't like that, at all. We weren't . . . criminy." He turned from me and kicked a brass-plated umbrella container near the front door. The metal cylinder and its rainy-day contents clattered cacophonously to the floor, then rolled across the hardwood, making a sound like thunder.

"By the way, I got a gander at your new restaurant downstairs," I noted, my rant picking up speed. "Cap's—as in *Caputo*? It's got a nice, selfish ring to it, Benny, ol' boy. How relieved you must have been to ditch your longtime encumbrance and finally strike out on your own. You got the broad, you got the business . . . hell, you hit the jackpot the day I was 'presumed dead.'"

Benny had still been trying to console Stella but as I said this, he turned to me, his features forlorn.

"If you want money from the old pizza place, I'll give you your cut, Nick. But Antonio's is gone. It was too painful for me to keep—"

"Painful? Oh, that's laughable. I don't want your money, you filthy, thieving crook!" Five years ago, this aspersion might have been a joke, part of our typical boyish banter. Today, this insult was meant to wound, and we all knew it.

"Ben, please don't let him upset you," Stella pleaded with him, softly. "Remember what the doctor said."

"Oh right," I scoffed. "His so-called 'fragile heart.' Don't worry about it, doll. Funny, doesn't it occur to anyone that *I'm* the guy whose ticker we should all be worried about right now? After all, *you* broke it, and your husband as good as plunged a dagger through it."

"Nick, what's happened is no one's fault! We've all been hurt by this!" Stella broke from Benny's embrace and tentatively approached me. "Benny and I were at our wits' end after we found out we had lost you. He picked up all of my crumbled pieces and I gathered up his busted shards, and we found a way to combine all those damaged remnants into a new life—together." As she spoke, I stepped over the wayward umbrellas and made my way to their framed wedding portrait, which I scrutinized more closely now. They looked like a duo you might see on a movie marquee, the prototypical Hollywood couple so self-possessed and effortlessly attractive. It made me sick. "Nick," Stella continued, "you're not the same person that you were when you left. Well, Benny and I aren't the same people, either. The war didn't just change you. It changed all of us. It changed everything."

She was right. The war had changed me. I thought back to the apprehensive and high-strung person I used to be. Benny had practically dragged me kicking and screaming onto that Sky Ride at the World's Fair. If he hadn't twisted my arm, Stella and I would never have crossed paths in the first place. Had she truly been destined for me, or had fate intended her to end up with Benny all along? My maelstrom of thoughts failed to dissipate the rage that had been slowly building, and this new reflection proved the capper. Thinking back to that day when we were kids, I suddenly realized that only one thing was going to make me feel better, so I walked over to my former friend and did it. I belted him, just the way he'd slugged me when we were twelve. Stella shrieked, and Benny reeled backward, grabbing at his jaw. The sound it had made upon impact with my fist let me know I had fractured it. He stumbled against the front door, knocking his head against the glass doorknob on his way to the floor. I reached down and picked him up by his collar. My intention had only been to move him out of the way, so that I could exit through the door, but Stella must have thought I was going to pummel him. She hurled herself onto my back, screaming for me to stop.

"Let go of me, Stella!" I shouted. She kicked and flailed and screamed, but would not let go of my neck. Still conscious, Benny's eyes looked up at me with a new sense of urgency. He was saying something, but over Stella's cries, I couldn't hear him. I yanked hard at her elbow, finally releasing the hold she had on me. The momentum of my arm movement sent her tumbling backward just as I finally deciphered what Benny had been groaning: "Don't hurt her, Nick!" he attempted to shout, his voice garbled by his own broken jaw. "She's pregnant!"

Thou Canst Not
Teach Me to Forget

GROUP HUGS WEREN'T EXACTLY MY FAMILY'S SHTICK, but on this, our last night of dinner service, Dad had called everyone together in the kitchen and told us to "huddle up." True to form, Frankie and Enzo were trying to stomp on each other's toes as we all stood encircled, arm in arm. Aunt Val was already crying, and my mom rubbed her back consolingly. On my right, Chef glanced at me with a bittersweet "this is it" expression, while Carmen, immediately to my left, had her eyes closed as if in prayer.

"You, too," said Dad, beckoning across the room to Mario, who was hanging back near the doorway.

"But guests are starting to filter in," he protested. "I should be at the front of the house."

"They can wait. Come on, ya big lug, get in here." Chef and I unclasped our arms to let Mario stand beside us.

"Don't forget the focaccia in the oven," Mario whispered to Chef as he joined us.

"It's never burned in the twenty-three years I've worked here— it won't burn tonight," Chef grumbled under his breath.

"Shhh . . . quiet everybody," said Enzo, suddenly a paragon of seriousness. "Uncle Benji wants to say something." Silence wasn't my family's forte, either, but in a rare moment of solemnity, everyone ceded the floor to my father.

"This is Cap's closing night on Taylor Street, as we all know," Dad began. "It's going to be tough to get through, but we still have a tradition to uphold. I want our patrons to get top-notch service, and, of course, remind everyone to spread the word about our new location. Val," he said, glancing at my aunt, "enough with the waterworks. Everyone needs to put on a happy face out there. Remember this isn't a tragedy; it's a celebration, of everything and everyone that got us here, and everything that's to come. My grandfather would be so proud of us—of the legacy we've managed to maintain, through good times and bad."

Dad's voice began to crack. Despite his pep talk, I couldn't help but wonder if he felt that he had failed his granddad. I looked around at the precious faces that hovered so close to mine. Only Ty—who was still recuperating at home, having just been released from the hospital—was missing. It was hard to believe what my father had just said. How was this a celebration? It sucked, plain and simple. This moment was the last of its kind. Life would go on—but not *this* life. "All right, everybody, that's all I've got, so let's wrap this up," Dad continued. "Let's get out there and do it. It's *ciao* time!"

"*Ciao* time!" we all repeated, with as much forced enthusiasm as we could muster.

As everyone returned to their duties, my mother approached Chef at the stove.

"Are you sure we can't convince you to come with us?" I heard her ask.

"If only I could," he said, shaking his head.

"I know it's wishful thinking," she said, placing a hand on his shoulder. "But I can't imagine the new Cap's without you. Other than Ben, you're the only one who—"

"—knows the family recipes?" Chef said. "You'd be surprised at what Val's boys have picked up from me over the years—Ty, in particular. They can pitch in at the stove, I'm sure of it."

"What will you do?"

"That I can't answer, yet. But I promise you, I'll be looking after Carmen, and the old Tin Man," he said, referring to the always stoic Mario. "And I know you'll take care of my Ladybird." He glanced at me from across the kitchen and winked.

With my heart hurting in my chest, I tied an apron around my waist and grabbed an order pad and pen from the pass-through before heading out into the dining room. Mario was already seating a few early-bird diners on the mezzanine, and as I glanced toward the front of the house, I was surprised to see a familiar face waiting by the door: the *Zwaggert* critic.

"Mr. Smith?" I said, rushing over to greet him. "How is your leg?"

He pulled up one leg of his trousers to reveal a limb now encased in a Velcro-trussed walking boot.

"Ahh, if it isn't my very own Florence Nightingale," he said. "Well, I'm on the mend. And I guess there's no harm in telling you now: My name's not Smith. I'm actually Nathan Davidson. Jason Smith is just the pseudonym I use on the job."

"We figured as much," I said. "So what brings you back to Cap's? Were all the water parks in your area closed? Because, you know, we can set up a Slip 'n Slide over by Table Ten if you're interested."

He laughed, which actually surprised me.

"I heard this was your closing night," he said. "I just wanted to come and pay my respects."

"Wow. Really? I thought you'd never want to step foot in here again, no pun intended. Isn't one broken leg enough?"

"Well, full disclosure, I wanted to have another go at that wild mushroom risotto, before it's too late," he said. "The best I've ever had."

"Are you serious? You actually *enjoyed* your meal?"

"Well, up until the Great Flood, of course. Food, service, ambience, history—you don't see a lot of family-owned restaurants like this in big cities anymore. Most dining experiences have gotten so corporate, and frankly, so culinarily tedious. Every new place seems driven more by trends and gimmicks than quality and classic flavor." His compliment left me slightly flummoxed. Deep down, I had always been proud of Cap's, but to hear it extolled by this objective expert—one who had no reason to sugar-coat his opinion—brought a glimmer of joy to this otherwise downer of a day.

"So, are you saying we might have made it into the next edition of *Zwaggert's*?" I asked.

"It was going to be a starred feature of the Chicago edition."

"That's great to hear, in a bittersweet sort of way," I said, pausing to reflect. "I don't suppose that you guys publish a Peoria edition?"

"Sorry, no. I do wish you folks the best down there, however. Peoria's lucky to be getting you, but Chicago is losing a real treasure." We both took a moment to glance around the dining room. I used to view our antiquated decor and menu—its veritable frozen-in-timeness—as a strike against us. But now, I could see how decades of history permeated the place like a pleasant patina on aging wood. If these walls could talk, as they say. There were ghosts in this room, and it was only too bad we couldn't box them up and take them with us.

"Well, anyway, it's going to mean a lot to my dad that you came by. I'll let him know you're here. I'm sure he'll want to say hello."

"He's got a lot of passion for his work, doesn't he?" the food critic asked as I started to turn away. I stopped in my tracks and glanced back at him.

"You don't know the half of it."

"I can tell," he continued. "I've been around this industry for a long time, and I've found that most places are only successful when the proprietors have their heart and soul invested in it. Even then, there are no guarantees. But if you don't *really* love it, you'll never make it in this business."

I nodded my assent, inwardly reflecting that my aspirations were lukewarm, at best. I loved Cap's, no doubt, but would I ever manage to summon up the requisite enthusiasm to operate it someday? In light of all the upheaval my family had been through in recent weeks, perhaps my own disinclination to carry on the family tradition was a moot point. They needed me now, more than ever, and as long as that was the case, I'd have to keep silent about the personal doubts I harbored.

* * *

"Gigi?" my dad called out, the next afternoon.

"In here," I shouted from the depths of Cap's storage room-slash-wine cellar, which, thanks to the poor lighting (a single low-watt bulb that dangled from the center of the ceiling) and my family's penchant for pack-rat behavior, resembled a dusty, underground catacomb. It was piled high with cardboard boxes, wooden crates, and file cabinets to one side and wine racks in varying states of disrepair to the other. Tattered work schedules and long-unused calendars hung haphazardly from thumbtacks on the dark wood-paneled walls alongside framed photographs and old Cap's menus with their elegant curlicue script and mind-bogglingly low prices. A black-and-white, institutional-style clock face that was forever stuck at nine o'clock confronted me accusingly from above the doorframe.

"Brought you this," my dad said, snaking his way through towers of half-packed boxes stacked near the door. He stepped over Sampson, who snoozed nearby on a pile of bubble wrap, and handed me a tumbler of water. Then he reached over to pluck a seemingly ancient bottle of wine from a metal wire shelf lining the wall. Turning the bottle over, he peered at the circular label affixed to the base. On it was written the owner's name and the date it had been left at Cap's for safekeeping. Years ago, before my cousins and I were born, patrons would bring pricey bottles of bubbly or wine for us to store for some future special occasion, like a birthday or anniversary, that they planned to celebrate at the restaurant. That was another era. Today's customers tended to favor instant gratification and, besides, our storage conditions weren't exactly up to current industry standards. That said, we still had a few bottles left over from Cap's glory days. Several belonged to formerly well-known Chicago politicians and sports figures—there was even a bottle of vintage Château Latour that had belonged to an alleged mafioso. Most of these VIPs likely weren't around anymore, but we still kept the bottles, just in case anyone ever showed up to claim them.

"Recycling bin?" I asked, deadpan.

"Very funny," he said. "You know I'd consider recycling Frankie or Enzo before I'd dump these babies." He replaced the bottle carefully back on the rack. "They're coming with us."

I couldn't figure out why Dad had saddled me with the almost Sisyphean task of sorting through and packing up this time capsule of what would soon be our former life. If he wanted to take my mind off the impending move, he couldn't have devised a more flawed plan. All I could think about was how my ancestors, who stared down at me from the sepia-tinted photographs on the wall, would probably have some choice Italian hand gestures for us if they knew we were abandoning everything they'd worked so hard to build.

"Why aren't we just tossing all of this other stuff?" I said, gesturing at the semi-sorted piles around me. "It's only some old letters, paperwork, and photos. I don't even know who most of these people are. How do I decide what we should keep and what we should pitch?"

"You know, I can't help but think of something my grandmother—your great-grandmother—used to always tell me," he said, leaning against the doorframe. "She used to say that hard work was the best and noblest distraction from anything . . . ." He paused and coughed uncomfortably.

"Painful?" I finished for him. Dad gave an affirmative shake of the head, and I knew he had a lump in his throat as big as the lump in mine. I went back to sorting to give us both a few minutes to regain our composure.

"Tell me what you're thinking about," he finally said. The request stunned me. My dad was *not* a "penny for your thoughts" kind of guy. He never had been, especially not where I was concerned.

"Nothing," I responded.

"I know that's not true," he said. "Look, I know you've always felt a little lost in the shuffle around here, but I want you to know that your opinion matters. It matters to me." I started to tear up. "See, I knew it," he continued. "Talk to me, baby."

"It's just that, well, we're . . . we're leaving *everything*. Who are we without this place? Who am *I*?" My dad sighed and gazed around the room.

"Gigi, even if it feels like we're leaving everything," he finally began, "I want you to understand that we're not. We'll always have the memories of Cap's, and we're taking those with us to—"

"Don't even say it," I interrupted, shaking my head. "It won't be the same."

"That's true. But it's like what Father Vito says about our bodies being the physical aspect of ourselves—'corporeal' is the word he used. The point is that we're more than that, because we have a spirit, too. Cap's is like that. It's a building, yeah, but the *spirit* of Cap's is so beyond any physical structure. It's the Caputos who were here before us," he said, waving his hand toward the remaining photos that were still on the wall. "And it's all of us, and the future Caputos: The kids you'll have someday, and their kids, too, God willing. I wanted you to see all this stuff, so that no matter what we leave behind, it's a part of your memory, a part of who you are. Nothing can ever change that. *Capiche?*"

I looked up at him and tried to answer, but my voice caught in my throat, so I just nodded. My dad bent down and kissed me on the forehead.

"I'm headed over to your Aunt Val's to help Frankie and Enzo finish packing up their place," he said, turning to leave. "Carmen's still lollygagging in the kitchen, so make sure you guys lock up when you leave. And don't be late for dinner. Your mom wants this last one to be special."

Not two minutes had passed before Carmen shuffled into the room with a conspiratorial look on her face, carrying the threadbare canvas tote bag she'd been bringing to work for as long as I could remember.

"I thought he'd never leave!" she said.

"Well, we should be going soon, too," I said. "I'm almost finished here."

"You're not going anywhere," she answered, winking at me.

"What are you up to?" I asked. For as blunt as she tended to be, the old lady was often surprisingly ambiguous.

"Here's the plan. I'll head over to the dinner at your place and will make up an excuse for why you're not with me."

"Huh? Why wouldn't I be there?"

"Because you'll be somewhere else . . . *with* someone else." She didn't need to be any more specific; the look on her face indicated exactly whom she meant.

"Carmen, stop. I told you already, it's over between Roman and me. We said our goodbyes weeks ago."

"But you have one more night."

"What's one more night in the big scheme of things?"

"Don't be so defeatist. One more night is everything. It's the whole universe," she responded.

"But I'm leaving."

"So?"

"So?" I responded, starting to become annoyed. "So it's a complete tragedy! And why do you have that goofy grin on your face? There is nothing happy about this situation whatsoever."

"You're alive. *That's* something to be happy about. You're young and beautiful. *That's* something to be happy about. You have a family that loves you, *and* a very charming boy who loves you, too. Don't you want to see him?"

"Of course I do! But what's the point?"

"It's Monday, and Monte's is closed. *Call* him. But before you do, add this to the boxes you're packing up." She reached into her tote bag and brought forth her treasured picture of my great-grandmother.

"But, Carmen," I protested. "You should keep this. It's yours."

"Pack it up with the rest," she said. "It belongs with your family. I have pictures enough in my memory—of all of you." Hearing her say this tore me in two. It was bad enough to leave behind my school friends and my first real love . . . but I was losing part of my family in this move, too. The hurt just kept on coming.

"I'm going to miss you so much," I said, leaning in to give her a hug.

"Not another word," she instructed. "You'll be a few hours away by car—not on the other side of the planet." She held me close for a moment and her small, bony frame felt frail in my arms. We didn't say a word to one another until she grabbed me by the shoulders and pushed me arm's length away from her. "I'm telling your parents that you'll be late for dinner. Whatever you decide to do with that time is up to you, but I advise you make the most of it."

When Carmen left, I contemplated everything she'd just said. The thought of seeing Roman again stirred up all those butterflies inside me that had only recently been subdued. To think that he and I might steal more time alone together sent a renewed electricity pulsing through my veins, but then, as if on cue, the storeroom went instantly black. The overhead light bulb had opted to blow out as if in a timely—or was it untimely?—show of solidarity. Rising to my feet, I navigated toward the still-lit hallway where I knew two wayward candles were sitting atop the credenza near the kitchen. I scavenged through the drawer underneath and found a half-used Cap's matchbook. I still hadn't decided whether to take Carmen up on her suggestion of contacting Roman. I needed more time to parse the pros and cons of such a move, and besides, I wasn't ready to leave Cap's just yet. I needed more time here before bidding my final farewell to the old place. Striking one of the flimsy matches, I lit the candles in their red beveled cups and headed back to the storage room.

"Out of my way, buddy," I said, using my knee to gently nudge the ever-oafish Sampson, who was standing between the boxes along my entry back into the glorified closet. His tail, as it thudded against the cardboard, seemed to be counting down the minutes we had left with its continual *thwap-swish! thwap-swish!* He followed me back to the center of the room and, after circling three times (as though performing intricate steps from an Elizabethan dance), came to rest on a pile of scattered papers and files on the floor.

I set the two candles on the corner of a box and remembered the photograph Carmen had brought me. Retrieving the hatbox of family photos I'd been packing up earlier, I removed the lid and peered inside. The faint, flickering light made the faces staring back at me take on an almost hallowed significance. There were many photos of my great-grandmother Stella: posed on a seventies-era floral sofa surrounded by a veritable litter of grandchildren; smiling graciously as she accepted some sort of chamber of commerce award; and, in a tarnished silver frame, a gorgeous wedding photo of her in a pearlescent silk gown with my dapper-looking great-grandpa Benito, Dad's namesake. God, she looked just like Grace Kelly. I picked up the framed photo Carmen had just left with me and saw that the tiny screws holding the black velvet matting in place were quite loose. I tried tightening them with my thumbnail, but within seconds, the backing gave way as if it had been waiting half a century for this moment. And there I found it: Tucked between the matting and the photograph was a yellowed envelope addressed to Dominick Monte. Dominick as in Nick Monte, Roman's great-grandfather? I carefully unsealed the envelope and slid the contents onto my palm. Folded within a handwritten, two-page letter was, unexpectedly, a baseball card. Holding the small cardboard image near the candlelight to inspect it more closely, I realized that it must be very old. I'd never heard of the player (his last name was Wagner), but he had ruddy cheeks, an insouciant smirk that reminded me of the *Mona Lisa*, and a head of dark hair parted down the middle. His collared Pittsburgh jersey was buttoned all the way up to his Adam's apple. I put the card down next to me and began to read the letter, deciphering the old-fashioned handwriting as best I could in the dim glow of the candles. My hands were trembling by the time I read the signature line. I carefully placed the letter and the baseball card back into the envelope for safekeeping before grabbing my phone. I didn't need Carmen's prodding; I had a *legitimate* reason to call him.

"Gigi?" Roman answered immediately. "Thank God. I was worried I wouldn't get to say goodbye."

"Hey, Roman," I said, my voice shaking with excitement, "I found something you need to see. I think it might be important. Can you come over now?"

"Of course. Where are you?"

"Cap's. Don't worry, I'm alone. How soon can you be here?"

"I'm right down the street. Be there in a few."

I set the phone down and picked up the envelope. It was almost weightless, yet it seemed to hold a lifetime within its small confines. Sampson must have sensed the urgency with which I'd spoken to Roman, because he'd bounded over and was prodding me excitedly, as if to ascertain that I was okay. In the process he upended a stack of old newspaper clippings I had already sorted into a pile on the floor.

"Sammy, watch out, honey—you're like a bull in a china shop over here." The words echoed almost in slow motion as I watched him back up gingerly at my command, just enough for his muscular tail to whack both of the candles that were propped on the box nearby.

I'd been trained in what to do in case of a fire, but as the piles of paper on the floor ignited I faced a disconcerting conundrum. The small blaze was just in front of the narrow aisle that led to the hallway, where the nearest fire extinguisher was located. Hopping over the flames to get to the hallway seemed the most obvious course of action, but then I noticed the still-full glass of water Dad had brought me earlier. Surely, this could quell the flames. I flung the contents of the glass at the growing conflagration, but the flames barely flinched. On the contrary, they seemed to increase in size. Sampson barked loudly and nuzzled the back of my knee hard, as though to march me toward the door, but the blaze was suddenly a few feet higher, feeding voraciously on paper and cardboard and . . . *the letter!* The envelope I'd discovered was lying on the ground just inches from the blaze. I felt the heat on my face as I bent to snatch it up, then hastily folded it in half and slid it into my back pocket. Unfortunately, there was no time to worry about saving any other mementos. The stockroom had become a perfect tinderbox, and, to my horror, my exit was now completely blocked. Pivoting on my feet, I rifled through a few nearby boxes on the floor, praying that we'd stashed some easily accessible tablecloths in it—anything with which I could smother the flames. No go. The fire was now triple the size it had been just ten seconds earlier. Samson was barking like a lunatic.

Call 911, I thought to myself. *No. Get out of here, first!* I ran to one of the imposing barricades of boxes near the door and tried to dismantle it, but the boxes were heavy and wouldn't budge. The smoke detector came screeching on as I looked to see if I could squeeze through any opening in the boxes and crates near the door. *Why wasn't the sprinkler system activating?* By now, the fire had advanced to the pile of bubble wrap on the floor and was giving off black, smoky fumes. Coughing, I lifted my shirt to cover my mouth but my eyes were stinging. I tried again to topple over the boxes in my path. A faint cold thrilled through my veins, even as I felt the heat of the fire consuming my family's cherished memorabilia. My lungs felt like they were equally ablaze with every hot and noxious breath I struggled to take.

"Gigi!" I heard Roman's voice call from somewhere far away. Was it real, or only imagined? I was beginning to feel incoherent, the mental equivalent of wading through a bog. Yet one tragic thought crystallized like a frantic signal flare in my brain: This was goodbye. I reached down, feeling for Sampson, and that was the last thing I remembered.

Beyond that, there was only a stifling emptiness—a strangely placid in-between place where thoughts and time ceased. I was as good as dead. There was nothing here, except . . . words? They started faintly at first, then louder, more urgently.

"Miss! Can you hear me?" I awoke not in an instant, but in fits and starts, as if being hoisted by a rope out of a deep, dark well. Blinking my eyes, I was startled to find myself lying on the pavement in the alley about a block away from Cap's, surrounded by a pair of EMTs and several other unfamiliar faces peering down at me with concern.

"Give her some room," said the one EMT, his voice terse as he removed an oxygen mask from my face and handed it to his partner. In my dazed state, only one thing registered in my brain.

"Roman?" I said with a rasp, trying to sit up. The EMT put a hand on my shoulder and gently prevented me.

"Careful," he warned. He was illuminated by flashing red lights that danced manically behind him. A crowd of people milled around in the periphery. I recognized a few as being other tenants of the building, residents who lived on the floors above Cap's.

"What happened? Is everyone okay? Where's Roman? He was supposed to be here," I said in rapid-fire succession.

A middle-aged woman in a red dress who had been staring at me with concern turned to the man next to her.

"She must mean the boy," she said gravely.

"What about him?" I wrestled my arm free from the blood pressure cuff the EMT had been trying to secure on me. The woman looked away, uncertainly, and nodded toward Cap's.

"I was coming down the back stairwell when I saw him bring you out," she explained. "He laid you on the ground, said something about a dog, and then bolted back inside." She shook her head, aghast, and brought both hands to her mouth in consternation.

"If he's not out by now, he's a goner," the man standing next to her bluntly observed.

I glanced down the alleyway and saw the lower portion of the building engulfed both in flames and an oppressive blanket of smoke. Picturing Roman somewhere in that hellish ruin sent a stabbing sensation ripping through my chest.

The ensuing minutes seemed like an eternity as firefighters, police officers, and EMTs swirled around me. Protesting, I was eventually strapped onto a gurney and swept into the back of an ambulance where, though safely out of the way, I couldn't see anything. Hearing what was happening but being unable to see it was more terrifying than witnessing it with my own eyes. The only thing I *could* see was the ominous reflection of the flames on the glass window of the ambulance.

"Roman!" I tried yelling, but my voice was a hoarse croak that barely lifted above a whisper.

CHAPTER 20

See What a Scourge Is Laid Upon Your Hate

THE PLACE NEEDED LOADS OF WORK, but I was up for the challenge. After all, what else was I going to do now that my life had been filched by my former best friend? Thanks to the recently approved G.I. Bill, easy money with laughably low interest rates flowed like cheap Chianti. Operating the pizza joint in Uptown had been the ideal dry run for opening up a bona fide restaurant, and besides, I had an agenda beyond merely making a living. So after hiring a crew to help me get my new venture off the ground, the first thing I did was put up the biggest, brightest neon sign I could fit over the street-facing front windows, with an appellation that was intended to taunt: Monte's.

The location was only three blocks away from Cap's on the Near West Side—exactly where I wanted to be. This wasn't just about stealing Benny's business or his thunder; I wanted my restaurant to serve as a constant reminder to him and Stella of their guilt and betrayal. No matter what trajectory the rest of their lives might take, Monte's would be there, looming in silent judgment.

"Where do you want these, buddy?" Two uniformed deliverymen showed up at the front door, wheeling in dollies that held large metal file cabinets.

"Take them down the hall to the first room on the right," I instructed. "My mother's in there getting the office all set up.

She'll show you where you can put 'em. And don't worry—her bark is worse than her bite."

Ma had scarcely left my side since I'd tracked her down in Cicero following my ill-fated encounter with Benny and Stella. If she was religious before I left for the war, she now doted on me like I was the risen Lord. Though at times I could sense from the look on her face that she was concerned about my dark moods and single-minded obsession with outdoing Cap's, she never voiced her reservations. The truth was, she was too overjoyed by my return from the dead to let any words of reproach escape her lips. For the first time in my life, I had a mother who was not only obliging, but downright obsequious. At times, I almost missed the old, overbearing Ma, but figured if anyone deserved to be kowtowed to, it was me.

"Excuse me, sir—I wanted to get your opinion before I painted any further." A neighborhood bobby soxer who was studying art at a nearby junior college had jumped at the chance to paint a large mural on the dining room wall. I glanced at her handiwork so far. "Do you like it?" she asked.

"*Cherubs?* You've got to be kidding me," I grimaced.

"You hate it," she said, a note of disappointment in her voice. The smudge of dark gray paint smeared right between her two brown eyes made her look as though she'd just come from an Ash Wednesday Mass. Her hair was tied up in a polka-dotted kerchief à la Rosie the Riveter. I hated the cherubs, it was true, but she seemed like a sweet kid. And she *was* working for free, I reminded myself.

"If it was good enough for the Sistine Chapel, it's good enough for Monte's. I want this place to be a little slice of heaven, after all," I said, trying to eke out an appreciative smile. "Now get back to work, Michelangelo."

"My name's Paula, but okay." She grinned at me, then returned to sizing up her masterpiece.

About two hours later, I was in the kitchen on my back, fitting a P-trap to the bottom of the new industrial-sized sink, when I heard the distinctive sound of women's heels on the tile floor.

"You still here, Ma? You ought to call it a day," I said, scooting out from under the counter. "Oh."

"Hello, Nick."

"What are *you* doing here?"

"The young woman in the front said you were back here." Even preceded by an ample pregnant belly, Stella was as beautiful as ever. The simple wool swing coat she wore did very little to conceal her condition, but she looked as radiantly wholesome as always. "I just wanted to let you know, after everything that has happened . . . ." She reached down and caressed her stomach contemplatively as she spoke. "Back when I first dated Benny, I used to call him Jell-O Head, because his curly hair had a life all its own. That hair was as animated and energetic as he was.'" She chuckled, still deep in thought. Jell-O? What on earth was she flapping her gums about? "When we thought you had died, he lost that particular verve. A certain stillness took over, as if all the vitality had been sapped from his body," she continued. "A part of him died the day we were told you were gone. And another part of him died when you came home, and, well . . . the look on your face . . . I'm really not sure you understand how much he . . . ." She sighed. "Oh, Nick, you meant the world to him."

"Yeah, well, talk about a funny way of showing it."

Stella began to weep. More waterworks? For crying out loud. "I really don't have anything to say to you, Stella." I tossed my rag and wrench onto the ground and got to my feet. "If you're mad about me opening up this place, well that's just tough cookies. It's a free country."

"*Nick!*" Stella's head reared back in horror as if what I had just said to her was a personal affront.

"Oh, come on. Don't act all sad and sanctimonious with me. Just move on. You're good at that." Stella looked at me in disgust.

"The service is Friday morning at nine. That's what I really came here to tell you. But please, do Benny and me both a favor and don't even think about showing up. And don't ever speak to me again." She turned in disgust and walked back out toward the front. Confused, I slowly followed her into what would soon be Monte's dining room and watched as she charged out the door and down the sidewalk. Paula, who was wiping her brush in a turpentine-soaked rag, joined me at the window.

"Poor lady," she said, shaking her head.

"Hardly," I scoffed.

"He was so young." I took my eyes off Stella crossing the street and turned back to the young artist.

"What are you talking about?" I asked.

"Her husband."

"What about him?"

"You haven't heard? Everyone within twelve blocks is talking about it."

Between busting my butt to get the restaurant off the ground and losing myself for days at a time in the mental equivalent of black holes, I hadn't exactly been front and center on the Taylor Street social scene. Needless to say, whatever Benny-related gossip was making the rounds hadn't yet made its way to me.

"What about her husband?"

"Oh, I figured you knew him. Seems like just about *everyone* loved that guy, the way people have been going on and on."

"Paula, what are you talking about?" I could feel my pulse quicken, and my knees felt like they might give out.

"That lady's husband, Benito Caputo—he died."

* * *

Hypertropic cardiomyopathy. That's the long-winded medical name of the heart condition those Army docs had been so worried about. Benny had collapsed without warning on the kitchen floor of Cap's restaurant. Ma had known for the past three days, only she hadn't been able to bring herself to tell me the news.

Reaching in my pocket for my father's watch on Friday morning, I glanced at the time: half-past ten. The funeral service at Our Lady of Pompeii would have concluded by now. I'd forbidden Ma from attending, but that hadn't stopped her from placing the newspaper obit directly next to the coffee pot before she left to run errands. (I'd stayed in bed until she'd gone to avoid any unsolicited discussion on the topic.) Though I barely skimmed the glowing remembrance, I couldn't help but take ironic note of the wedding date listed for Benny and Stella: September 1, 1945. I'd been liberated from the camp on August 27, just five days earlier.

Months ago I had managed to get to the bottom of the missing telegram—the one that had made a mockery of my entire life by failing to materialize. Following persistent inquiries with the local Western Union office, the telegram was finally discovered wedged between the wall and a desk in the office, having apparently slipped there, unseen, instead of being routed on with all of the other outgoing messages. It had never been reported as undelivered because it had vanished into thin air. A single piece of paper, blown out of sight by the faintest breeze, had prolonged Ma's anguish by four needless months, and had allowed an oblivious Benny and Stella to meet at the altar.

Was the mislaid telegram really to blame? Not if I was being honest with myself. Stella loved Benny, just as the whole world had loved him. Of course I was saddened by the news of Benny's death. Yes, I felt numb. But it wasn't because he was gone. He had been dead to me the moment I realized he was capable of the most selfish act imaginable. Now, I only felt loss, sadness, and, I'll admit it, anger. The fact that so much of my life had been spent worshipping at the feet of a man who had charmed even himself into thinking that he was a good person filled me with disgust.

The guy whose catchphrase had been "trust me" had turned out to be the last person on the planet I ought to have trusted.

Stella was no better. The cynical side of me had one possible explanation for her having come round to the restaurant earlier in the week. Now that she was pregnant and alone, I reckon she took me for an appealing fallback plan, just like the last time Benny had ditched her. Nick Monte, forever doomed to be second at bat. It was a horrible thing to assume of a grieving widow, but I couldn't help myself—if I thought the worst of Benny and Stella, they had only themselves to blame.

Ma turned the key on the side door leading in off the alley and walked through the short hallway into the kitchen, placing her pocketbook next to the toaster. She was wearing her black boiled wool pillbox hat, most unsuitable for May.

"Did you leave the groceries downstairs?" I asked her, rising to go fetch them. "I told you to just have them delivered."

"I didn't go to Goldblatt's, Dominick." She unpinned her hat and set it on the counter. Her eyes were red and puffy. "The church was more crowded than I've ever seen it—put even Christmas and Easter attendance to shame. People were spilling out onto Lexington Street."

"Tell it to your coffee klatch—I'm not interested in hearing another word about it," I groused, clearing my breakfast dish from the table.

"You most certainly *will* hear about it, young man," she said, sounding more like her old, no-nonsense self than she had since my return. "I've been walking on tenterhooks around you for months, and it ends today."

"Boy, maybe I ought to have taken my chances and stayed back in the prison camp," I said, my face beginning to feel flushed.

"Just stop it. I've had enough of watching you drown in your own pity. It's time to wake up. Life is for the living."

"My apologies, Mother. Being starved, tortured, and written off for dead by everyone who's ever known you does funny things to people."

"Well, I've had enough of it. Enough of your anger, your bitterness, your sarcasm, and your moping around. You survived, whether you like it or not, and you should thank your lucky stars for it. How can you joke at a time like this? It's like spitting on the grave of your father, not to mention your oldest friend."

"Benny's not my friend, but spitting on his grave? Now that's not a half bad idea."

"Shame on you, Dominick Monte!" she snapped. "Shame on you!"

"No, Ma!" I shouted back, rising from the kitchen chair. "Shame on him!"

I stormed out of the room and through the side door, descending the wooden staircase. Its creaky treads were too narrow for my size ten feet. I hated this new apartment, and as I started walking down the sidewalk, it occurred to me that I had no good retreat here. In my former life, I would have climbed out onto the fire escape after a row with Ma, or found sanctuary in Benny's bedroom across the hall. Those obviously weren't options anymore. I was in exile now, living a nightmare that felt as though it would never conclude. Ma wasn't the first person to have told me to wake up and open my eyes. Benny had said that to me the day I met Stella. It's what had convinced me to go up on that Sky Ride at the fair in the first place. Well, I'd woken up, all right. My eyes had been opened. And what I saw was heartache, disappointment, and the realization that the two people I loved most in this world had loved each other more.

Never again. I was never going to be able to reflect on my childhood with any sort of fondness. Recollections of my first love would only fill me with animosity, not affectionate nostalgia. Hearing the name Caputo was a curse to me now, and I vowed to make anyone and everyone who would listen to me understand that. People may have flocked to Benny's funeral, but he was no saint. He was no friend. The world could sing his praises, but I knew the truth, and I would rather malign his memory than pretend to mourn his death.

I paused at the corner of Taylor and Lytle. My breathing was labored and I glanced toward the cerulean-blue sky as my eyes stung from the effort of fighting off tears. *Damn it, Nick Monte. Stop. Don't you dare let him do this to you, too. Not after everything else. He's not worth it.* He'd been my best friend when I was young and stupid and couldn't tell the devil from a dollar bill. He was my friend once, but I would *never* call him friend again. Ever.

CHAPTER 21

Two Households, Both Alike in Dignity

"LADYBIRD—ARE YOU DOING OKAY IN THERE?" Chef asked, his voice gentle as he tapped on my bedroom door. I opened it and let him see the dress I'd finally chosen to wear, having already anxiously discarded a host of others that now formed a small mountain on my bed.

"Is the black too . . . I don't know—*somber*?" I asked. "I've never gone to something like this before. I guess I still can't believe it's even happening."

Sensing from my voice that I was in full freak-out mode, Chef placed one kitchen-scarred hand on my shoulder and kneaded it like the many hunks of pizza dough that came before.

"I know, kiddo," he said, slowly shaking his head. "It's beyond surreal. Don't worry, I think anything you wear would meet Roman's approval, and that's all that's important." I sighed and walked to my closet to grab a purse.

"I just keep replaying that night over and over in my head," I said, gazing blankly out the small dormer window that looked onto the street below. "I wouldn't be here right now if he hadn't . . . ."

"We'll always be grateful," Chef interrupted, refusing to let me dwell on the recent incident. "It's why your parents—even your cousins—will be there today, as a sign of our family's appreciation for what he did. Your folks have already headed over. I hate to rush you, but I think we should try to get there soon, too. Make sure things stay friendly."

"I hardly think anyone would use a day like this as an opportunity to reignite the feud," I said, blanching at my own metaphor.

"Normally I'd agree, but having Caputos and Montes in the same room together? It's going to be more than a little tense. Who'd have ever thought it would take something so horrific for the families to call a truce—*if* you can even call it that. Just remember: Roman's parents want this to be a celebration."

I opted not to respond, certain that if I let myself register even an ounce more of emotion, the floodgates would open and my tears would float us all the way to Peoria. Instead, I glanced inside my purse to make sure I had everything I needed, including enough tissues to see me through this final goodbye.

Within the half hour, Chef and I had entered through Monte's stained glass front doors, on which, hanging from a black grosgrain ribbon, was a sign that read, "Closed for a private event." Once inside, a stoic-looking older man in a dark suit escorted us to a large room at the back of the restaurant normally used for weddings and birthday parties.

"Are you ready for this?" Chef whispered. He squeezed my hand as we paused on the threshold to take in the mostly unfamiliar faces, many of whom were engaged in hushed conversation.

"Um, I think so?" I replied in an indecisive mumble, trying to spot anyone remotely recognizable. "There they are," I said, at the same moment realizing I'd been holding my breath. I slowly exhaled and tried to calm my racing heart. Aunt Val and my parents were standing with Roman's parents, Joe and Peggy, at the far end of the room. Frankie and Enzo hovered just a few feet away, and it looked as though they were entertaining some of the smaller members of the Monte clan with their "how'd this quarter get in your ear?"

trick. Chef's initial fears aside, I felt a sudden sense of relief that my relatives had arrived first. I'd lately been so busy lamenting all the ways I didn't fit in that I'd forgotten to appreciate how great it felt to know they were always there for me, including on a day like today. I remembered what my dad had been trying to tell me on the night of the fire. Now I truly understood.

I eventually noticed Ty slumped at the far end of a long table. He flicked his forefinger morosely at the leaves of a floral centerpiece. We hadn't really gotten a chance to talk alone since he'd been released from the hospital, and I suspected he'd been avoiding me. Maybe a crowded room was the perfect place to start the conversation we so desperately needed. I left Chef with Carmen, who had just arrived in her Sunday best, and walked over to my cousin.

"Mind if I sit?" I asked him, as he glared sullenly into his water glass.

"Sure," he said, finally meeting my eyes as I took a seat next to him.

"Your silence is deafening."

"I'm here, aren't I?"

"Yes, you are, and thanks for that," I said. "I know it can't be easy. Even if Aunt Val made you come, I want you to know that—"

"No one made me come," he said, stopping me mid-sentence. "He saved your life, Gigi. Don't think that doesn't mean anything." Seeming to lose track of what he wanted to say next, Ty glanced intently over my shoulder. I turned to follow his gaze, as the other guests in the room murmured excitedly at the elderly man in a wheelchair who had just made his grand entrance. Over his lap was a wool blanket, and on top of that, his gnarled hands gripped a wooden cane.

"Grandpa Monte! What on earth—" Mrs. Monte's hand reached up to cover her open mouth, but she dropped it again to utter a confused, "Roman?"

"Hey, Mom," my rescuer of late replied, as he pushed his great-grandfather's wheelchair into the center of the room. "Hope it's okay that I brought one more guest. The nursing staff said it would be fine, as long as we kept him away from the Sambuca." The old man glowered as a few people chuckled. Finding my face in the crowd, Roman raised his eyebrows in an "all systems go" sort of way, and I tentatively waved back. Here went nothing.

In the midst of all the confusion on the night of the fire, I hadn't known until well after the fact that my erstwhile beau had escaped the building—with Sampson in tow—before the conflagration could claim either of them. Roman was treated for minor burns and smoke inhalation by another team of medics on the street in front of the building and was taken, by separate ambulance, to the same hospital where I had been admitted. Our parents encountered each other in the waiting room, and in her gratitude to Roman for saving my life, my mom had tentatively extended an olive branch to his mother. Mrs. Monte responded in kind by suggesting a détente in the form of a going away party for the Caputo family, hosted at Monte's. And so here we all were, attempting to do the unthinkable: break bread with one another despite a history of acrimony and ill will that spanned beyond three-quarters of a century. Roman's heroics may have saved my life, but it was hardly going to transform so much venom and hatred into instant sunshine and lollipops. My father and cousins had grudgingly agreed to attend this improbable soiree for my mother's sake, and Roman said that many in the Monte family were similarly skeptical. Perhaps that's the reason why he and I had decided to make this last-ditch attempt to end the hostility by addressing what had started it all. Great-Grandpa Monte was our unwitting pawn in all this, but now, seeing how frail he was, I fervently hoped we weren't making a very grave mistake despite our very best intentions.

Roman wheeled his family's patriarch over to me, and I bent down to say a tentative hello. Everyone in the room watched in quiet anticipation, but words eluded me. Dominick Monte, though he looked severe and intimidating, sensed my hesitation and spoke first.

"You must be Gigi," he said. "Those eyes . . . I haven't seen blue eyes like yours since . . . well, let's just say it's been a long time. Roman says you found something that belongs to me?"

"Yes," I said, standing back up. "A letter. It appears to have been misplaced."

"Letters gone AWOL. Wouldn't be my first go-round with that," he mused, more to himself than for anyone else's benefit.

"It would be charcoal right now—and so would I, I guess—if it wasn't for your great-grandson, sir," I added, glancing at Roman with a faint smile.

"I'm not sure if running into a burning building *twice* makes him intrepid or an idiot. A little of both, I reckon. But for your sake—and your family's—I'm glad he got you out of there."

As my family and the Montes gathered around, I opened my purse and nervously pulled out the envelope I'd found in the old picture frame. I tried to hand it to Mr. Monte, but he refused to take it. "My eyesight isn't what it once was," he explained. "Why don't you read it to me?"

"Aloud? Are you sure?" I asked. "It's sort of private."

"At my age, there's not much you could say that would embarrass or shock me, young lady," he grumbled. I looked at Roman who gave me an encouraging nod. Removing the letter from the envelope, I unfolded it, and after glancing quickly at the expectant faces of our two families, I took a deep breath and began to read:

April 28, 1946
Dear Nick,
I wanted to tell you this in person, but that seems to be impossible since you're refusing to see me. Not that I blame you. I know what this must look like. You come home, a genuine, honest-to-God war hero, only to find that I've married your girl. Those are the facts, and there's no disputing them, so I'm not even going to try.

I paused and looked at Mr. Monte. His hand trembled slightly as he waved at me to continue.

But Nick, here's the thing: I know you're angry, and you have every right to be. Angry at the war. Angry at the world. And angry at me. I took your Stella. The Stella you loved since you were twelve. That's right. I know—and I knew. When I realized my Estelle was your Stella, I gave her up, because I promised you I'd find her for you all those years ago. And unbeknownst to me, I had found her. I played the fickle Don Juan in tossing her aside, but it was all an act, because I loved her, too. I'm no saint, but breaking it off with her was the hardest thing I've ever done. When we thought you were dead—Nicky, we knew you were dead—it seemed like the right thing to do. Hell, it seemed like the only thing to do. I would never have touched her or told either of you how I felt if things had been different. You have to know that, Nick. If there's any love left in your heart for Stella, and if our friendship—yours and mine—still means anything to you, you have to forgive us. If not me, then at least forgive Stella. She's innocent in all this. She loved you, and, as a matter of fact, I'm certain she loves you still. It was always you for her. She'd never tell me so, but I'm not as stupid or callous as people think; marrying me was her way of staying connected to you. I knew that, and yet I chose to live with it. That's how much I love her. I wanted to take care of her, to make her happy. If you can believe it, I thought it's what you would've wanted.

I looked up again. Tears had welled up in Nick Monte's eyes. "There's more?" he asked. I nodded. "Go on, then."

There's something else you ought to know, another reason you must find it in your heart to forgive Stella. Those docs tell me I'm not going to be around much longer. I need you to be there for her . . . and for our child. I can't bear to leave her without knowing this is settled, so please tell me I can count on you to help my family. I'm humbly asking you, in the name of the friendship we once had, and in the name of the love you have for Stella, to move past your anger. There's not much time. Please come and see us soon. We need you.

Love,
Benny Caputo

"Grandpa Benny?" Aunt Val whispered, aghast. "He and Grandpa Benny were *friends*?"

"There's a postscript," I said. "It reads, 'P.S. You told me to keep this for you, but I think it's time I gave it back.'" I pulled the baseball card from the envelope and handed it to Mr. Monte, who stared down at it for a long time without uttering a word.

"Ty, you've got to check this out," Enzo finally said, his voice registering something akin to awe as he leaned over the elderly man's shoulder. "Is this what I think it is?"

My oldest cousin slowly inched around me and stood next to his brother to get a glimpse at the long-lost treasure. In an instant, his face also gave way to disbelief.

"Honus Wagner," he marveled.

"The one and only," Roman said, joining my two cousins. "I got chills when Gigi first showed it to me."

"Honus who?" asked my mom, confused.

"Let's just say this is the Hope Diamond of baseball cards," explained Roman.

"Make that the Holy Grail—at least where collectors are concerned," Ty added. For a moment, at least, the two young men had seemingly forgotten their subway station fracas, jointly mesmerized, as it were, by this piece of sports memorabilia.

"Looks like it's in semi-decent condition," added Frankie, joining his twin brother. "If that thing's real, we're talking *crazy* money. Six figures, at least."

"More than that, young man. It's worth more than you could ever imagine," Nick Monte replied, his voice husky. "As a matter of fact, you could say it's priceless . . . to me, at least."

I'm not exactly sure what Roman and I had expected would happen after we delivered that letter, so many years after it had been written. I guess a part of me hoped it might instantly tie up our families' relationship into some nice little bow, the way things conclude so perfectly in the last five minutes of a feel-good movie. But as Roman's mother escorted Mr. Monte to the head of the table for the ensuing dinner, that didn't happen. Instead, life simply went on. It went on the same way things always did in the lives of Italian families: with food. From out of the Montes' kitchen came steaming pots of pasta puttanesca, platters of meatballs and veal scallopini, Caprese salad and plates of charcuterie, which we all dined on, family-style, at the one long table in the room. The tone of the dinner, though stilted at first, eventually loosened up (the adults helped along, I suspect, by the dwindling carafes of Chianti dotting the table). Roman and I each did our part to make introductions and usher the conversation along where we could. Talk eventually turned from polite pleasantries to the common ground we all shared as fixtures on Taylor Street. As we exchanged anecdotes about our families and the neighborhood, the stories made me wistful about having to abandon it all. My cousins and Roman's younger siblings debated the best flavors at Mario's Italian Lemonade while my dad and Joe Monte got all starry-eyed singing the praises of Chiarugi Hardware. Roman's mom and mine discovered they had attended the now long-gone Notre Dame parochial school within a few years of one another, and even Chef could be heard trading cooking tips with Roman's grandmother, Marie. Curiously, I noticed that Carmen had pulled her chair next to Roman's great-grandfather and the two senior citizens huddled in private conversation throughout much of the meal as if they were somehow making up for lost time.

"That's quite a mural you folks have out in the front dining room," my dad finally said over a dessert of profiteroles.

"My beautiful wife, Paula, painted that many years ago, God rest her soul," said Dominick Monte. "Mr. Caputo, I've got to say, I'm truly sorry to hear of the troubles you've had with your restaurant."

"Call me Ben. Yes, it's safe to say the last few years have been difficult," Dad said. Oh, no. Dinner had gone so well. Did we really need to end things on this note? No one reflected on the fact that the Caputo/Monte feud was partly to blame for Cap's Taylor Street demise. But based on the silence at the table, one had to suspect it was on everyone's minds.

"The fire," Roman's dad said, joining the conversation with a note of tactful condolence, "what's the toll, damage-wise?"

"It was mostly confined to the back areas: the stockroom, office, and kitchen," my dad answered. "The front of the house, which we just renovated a few months ago, was largely spared. Not that it matters. I imagine the next owner will opt for a complete gut and redo, anyway. Damn useless sprinkler system. If that fire wasn't a signal it's time for we Caputos to move on, I don't know what is." He sighed, then swallowed the last dregs from his wine glass in defeat.

"And on that note," said my mother, taking her cue from my dad's chagrined expression, "I think we Caputos have probably reached the limits of your hospitality. Gigi, shall we help clear the plates before we say our goodbyes?"

I rose from my seat to begin collecting the silverware—even as one of the honored guests at this event, my inner waitress lived on.

"Not so fast, young lady," said Dominick Monte, reaching out one of his palsied hands to stop me. Though he'd been nothing but kind to me, I suddenly felt another flash of fear and trepidation course through my veins. "You've dredged up my past with that letter of yours," he said, "so what do you have to say about it?"

"I . . . um . . . excuse me?" I stammered, confused and a little bit terrified.

"I've been watching you all through dinner," he continued, "and I can tell by the look on your face that you have something on your mind, something you would like to say but are keeping to yourself. I know that because, well, I've spent most of my life wearing a similar expression."

"I'm not sure I understand what you mean," I said, feeling more than a little discomfited.

"Have you ever heard the saying, *parlare fuori dai denti*?" he asked, his tone gentler. I shook my head. "The English equivalent would be 'speak your mind.'"

My face flushed hot, and I glanced at the table, suddenly feeling as if I might collapse.

"Gigi?" my mother asked. "Is everything okay?"

"It was my fault," I blurted out, my voice beginning to crack. "The fire. I'm the one who destroyed Cap's. It's all because of me."

"Honey, no! It was an accident," Mom said.

"If anything, it was Sampson," Frankie pointed out, trying feebly to help.

"Sweetheart, nobody blames you," my dad reassured me. "We had already said our goodbyes to the old place, and like I told you before, the building doesn't matter. *You're* the future of Cap's."

"You don't understand," I said, shaking my head. "That's just it. I'm not!" I sighed and gently placed the fistful of forks I'd been collecting back down on my dessert plate. "You've been preparing me for it my whole life. It's been your dream, but I don't know if Cap's . . . is *my* dream." My dad looked at me, not so much angry as confused.

"I thought running the restaurant—taking it over from me someday—I thought that's what you wanted."

"I'm sixteen, Dad. I have no earthly clue what I want from my future." I wiped at a tear that had sprung up in my eye. "Your expectations of me—I'm really sorry, but it's just all too much." I didn't want to let my father down. I didn't want to hurt *anyone*. But I finally had to acknowledge the truth. As I said the words, it felt like opening a long-locked door with a newly discovered key. I was way too young to have "found my passion," as people say, but I knew I had just found the one thing that would help me, some day, to figure it all out: my *voice*.

"Okay," Dad said. "Tell me what you *do* want. I'm listening."

I wasn't even sure how to respond to his question until I glanced down at Roman, who was still seated beside me. The look in his eyes gave me my answer.

"I want *him*," I said, reaching to grab for his hand. "We love each other, and we don't expect any of you to understand that, but we're not going to hide it anymore. I can't change the fact that we're moving away. And I can't change the past. But Roman and I—we can change the future. Our future." I paused, and turned to Roman. "I won't give you up. I know I would always regret it." I stopped speaking, suddenly flushed with embarrassment. Roman stood up and put his arm around my shoulders.

"Me, too," he whispered into my ear. My declaration of independence seemed to hang in the air like a gauntlet that had just been thrown down. No one wanted to be the person who broke the ensuing silence. But at last, Dominick Monte did.

"My best friend and I started our pizza joint when we were just about your age," he said, addressing Roman and me. "That was our dream—Benny's and mine—but I know I can speak for him when I say that it was never intended to be your burden."

"Of course not, Gigi," my Dad said softly.

"So many memories have been reawakened for me today. Some wonderful," Mr. Monte continued, glancing fondly at Carmen, "and some very painful. You've reminded me, Gigi, of something your great-grandfather Benny once told me." He brought the tips of his fingers together and tapped them thoughtfully. "He said it was the things we *didn't* do that we'd regret. My greatest regret turned out to be not making things right between us before he died, especially since all the anger that drove me for so many years finally shriveled up and blew away. One day I woke up, and it was just . . . gone," he said, waving one hand as though he were brushing away invisible cobwebs. "Letter or no letter, I *should* have taken care of Benny's family when he died. I didn't. Instead, I launched a feud that has hurt so many people." He paused as if to catch his breath, but instead his head slumped forward and his shoulders began to shake. I couldn't see the tears—he kept one timeworn hand cupped across his face, hiding what could only have been decades of pent-up emotions. Aside from the sound of his quiet sobs, there was a deferential silence in the room. It was clear to everyone that we were collectively witnessing a profound and deeply personal moment. Releasing his grip on my hand, Roman approached his great-grandfather's wheelchair, knelt, and sweetly placed one arm over the old man's convulsing shoulders.

As if at the insistent urging of some mysterious outside force, I felt compelled to join them and rushed to kneel opposite Roman at Nick Monte's side. I gripped the arm of his wheelchair, uncertain of what I should say or do next, when the old man clutched my hand and Roman's and joined them both firmly in his.

"It ends here, today," he told us in a barely audible murmur. "It ends with you."

And the Rank Poison
of the Old Will Die

"ORDER'S UP!" Ty shouted over the din, sliding it onto the new pass-through ledge and slamming his hand down—*ding!*—on the old-fashioned call bell.

Standing nearby, I instinctively reached to grab the bowl of steaming hot *cioppino*, planning to deliver it to Table Seven.

"Uh-uh. Not tonight, you don't," Mom said, swooping in front of me to retrieve the dish.

"Mom, seriously, I can do it," I said, shaking my head in comic frustration.

"And spill something on your dress before your date even arrives? No way."

"You're off duty, Gigi," Dad yelled to me from across the dining room as he escorted a family of five—future loyal customers, we could only hope—to their table.

This wasn't the old Cap's. It was something else entirely. I glanced contentedly at surroundings that still seemed slightly unfamiliar. Standing as placid as a pillar in the midst of this strangely comforting commotion, I felt centered. Grounded. The days, months, and years ahead were pages of an unwritten book; I had no earthly idea where my life would eventually take me, but of one thing I was certain: This was home. Like a phoenix rising from the ashes, our family business had been reborn, and in many ways you could say the same thing about me. So much had changed. And therein lay the most ironic part of it all: The only thing that *hadn't* changed was . . . our address.

"Hey, Chef, where's my veggie deep-dish?" said Frankie, stashing his order pad in his apron and shoving his pen behind his ear.

"It's coming up right now—you can't rush perfection," called that old familiar voice from the kitchen as Mario, grabbing more menus from behind the bar, stopped long enough to remark, "It's pizza, not *The Last Supper*."

It hadn't been easy for my father to accept Dominick Monte's offer. The last thing Dad wanted was to be considered a charity case, especially by our one-time sworn rivals. But Roman's great-grandfather insisted that he was going to cash in Honus Wagner, and he argued that if our family refused a portion of the remittance, we'd be depriving him of his chance to atone with God. That kind of name-dropping trumps everything for Roman Catholics, which is why my parents eventually yielded. The generous check from Mr. Monte erased my family's money problems in an instant. Dad paid Rich Beresdorfer back his loan plus interest, leaving the vulture to go conduct his business elsewhere. Though the insurance company had balked on covering the damages at Cap's because of the malfunctioning sprinklers, it didn't matter. We had money enough to rebuild from the fire damage *and* cover all of Ty's medical bills.

Cap's was closed nine months for renovations, giving me just the break I needed to take stock. I concentrated on school, my friends, and, of course, Roman. By the time the business reopened, I really missed the restaurant and was glad to be back in the swing of things with our new and improved digs. Still, my folks—seeing how much happier I was with more time for myself—decided to dramatically curtail my shifts. Roman's parents—not wanting to see him suffer the same level of burnout that I had—had become equally liberal with his time off.

"Is he here yet?" Carmen asked on her way to give a table their bill. "Where are you two lovebirds heading tonight?"

"I'm not sure. He told me it's a surprise," I said. I glanced over at the hungry crowd now converging on Mario near the front entrance to see if there was any sign of him yet. Just at that moment the door opened, and, backlit by the late afternoon sun, I saw him. He slipped through the door, much as he had the night of my sixteenth birthday, but this time he was a welcome guest. We locked eyes, and my heart gave that same hiccup it had when we first met. This time, we made our exit together, hand in hand.

The sun was just beginning to make its descent as we ambled down Taylor Street to our mystery destination. Turning right onto Loomis Street we entered Arrigo Park, the site of our secret tryst on that hot day last summer.

"Returning to the scene of my sob fest?" I teased, nudging my shoulder against his as we entered the park.

"Just wait—we're not there yet," he said, giving my hand a squeeze.

Near a patch of sycamore trees, Roman led me down a narrow gravel walkway. I gasped when we got to the end of the short trail.

"It's beautiful!"

"They put the last of the plantings in today," Roman explained. "It's all been done exactly to the specifications that he left in his will." The sun's setting rays shone through the surrounding trees, casting an almost magical light in the small fern-dotted glen. A solitary granite bench, big enough to seat two, was situated at the center of the small garden. I approached it to read the inscription that had been etched upon it with gold inlay:

From gloom and woe let peace and friendship grow.
—In loving memory of Dominick Monte and Benito Caputo

Roman and I took a seat on the bench, and I rested my head upon his shoulder. In the trees above us, a nightingale—or was it a lark?—sang sweetly.

The End